VALKYRIE

GUARDIAN SECURITY SHADOW WORLD

KRIS MICHAELS

Created with Vellum

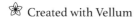

1

Author's Note: This book takes place in the late summer-early fall before Frank's story is told at Christmas.

VALKYRIE GAZED out of the window as the chauffeur-driven car sped through the dark cloak of night. Morning was still a few hours away. New York had finally settled into a state of semi-consciousness. While the city didn't sleep, it fell into a fugue state between three in the morning and dawn.

She rubbed her hands together, removing the nerves that were building. *Damn it, woman. Get a grip.* Yet her mouth was dry, and her stomach flipped like an acrobat on a trapeze. She was a veteran of some of the most demanding missions imaginable. She'd done and seen things that would decimate lesser people. Yet, this ... Well, it was a new type of mission for her.

Perhaps mission wasn't exactly the correct word. True, she'd been actively planning this particular event for almost three months and playing with the idea for much longer. The entire situation had the tactical components, which required stealth, skill, and a metric fuck-ton of detailed coordination. *Let's not forget guts.*

Right. Guts. She rolled her eyes and sighed. She had that trait. There was absolutely no doubt about that fact. Her intestinal fortitude had pushed her through losing her late husband, the grueling training to become an assassin, and the continued missions for Guardian.

No matter what Guardian threw at her, losing her husband would always be the most challenging thing she'd ever done. He'd been dead for ten years, and she still missed him but had let the hatred and anger go. She'd grown and moved forward.

Forward into a world of utter darkness. Guardian had trained her to make her way in environments no decent human ever saw. Now, as the assassin Valkyrie, she used her body to tempt and ensnare some of the world's most powerful and hated men. Assassination and the allure of sex went hand in hand for her. That play, the suggestion of sex—and sometimes the actual act—gave her the advantage. She'd utilize anything within her realm of influence to complete a mission.

Yet, she was taking a calculated risk on her newest op. Not necessarily making herself vulnerable, but it was as close as she'd come to opening that door. A door she'd decided months ago she needed to open again. Vulnerability allowed for weakness. The last time she was weak was the night she'd grieved over her husband's dead, battered body. That night, she'd discovered that the cage match her husband had died fighting in was rigged. He'd been drugged because he refused to throw a fight to clear the debt he owed. Her husband was addicted to gambling. He'd lost everything they owned and, at the end, he'd lost her respect. But she still loved the man she'd married.

His addiction had finally killed him, but not the way she'd thought it would. The trainer had seen it happen. Something rubbed onto the other fighter's taped fists. A clench was all that was needed to deliver the drug, and then the other fighter beat her husband to death. The ref let the match continue even though her husband couldn't lift his hands.

Val went after everyone involved and those who benefited from her husband's murder. Her husband's agent and promoter partner bet against her husband, who was the favorite to win the match. They'd raked in the money. She'd tracked and killed everyone starting at dawn on the one-month anniversary of her husband's death. She took out the ref, the fighter, his trainers, and the promoters. Unfortunately, she hadn't looked for or seen the camera in the office. The police arrested her, and while she waited for trial, Demos came to see her. The recruiter for Guardian didn't pull any punches when he explained why he was there. She had a decision to make, there on the spot. No time to think, no time to waver.

She'd agreed to the job's terms and expectations and walked out of that jail with her new mentor. Her face was altered, and her education was enhanced. She'd learned to speak three languages fluently and was working on another. Money was never a concern since starting work for

Guardian. To anyone looking from the outside in, she was the consummate socialite. She lived in a beautiful world.

But there was one problem. Valkyrie, the assassin, the trained killer, was bone-shatteringly lonely—until recently. There was a place inside her that needed personal contact with another human. She had a few friends, but she was cautious to keep them at arm's length even as she pretended to let them in. Phoenix, Ice, Harbinger, Malice, Flack, Smoke and Reaper were in that tiny circle. But she wanted, no, craved more. That was a secret she'd never tell a soul. It was a secret that could be exploited, and she'd never put herself in that position again. Never.

She glanced up at the building they were passing. "This is it. Pull over." Her driver, a member of Guardian Security who she'd borrowed from the New York office for the early morning logistical assist, glanced at the building and then back at her. "Are you sure?"

She nodded. "Pull over here and wait for me."

"Are you armed, ma'am?" The man glanced around the neighborhood. "Perhaps I should accompany you?"

Valkyrie rolled her eyes. *As if*. "I'm good.

Thanks." She waited for the man to open her car door and exited the vehicle. Her Louboutin heels, Prada slack suit, silk shirt, and white crocodile Niloticus Himalaya Hermes Birkin purse belonged in a penthouse in Manhattan, not in one of the poorest boroughs in the city. She stepped across the stained and litter-strewn sidewalk.

There it was. But ... She could turn back, and no one would ever know. "You would," she said quietly before carefully stepping down the broken and cracked concrete stairs to the basement apartment.

"Just do what you came here to do," she muttered. Drawing in a breath, she squared her shoulders and knocked on the door. She listened carefully, not knowing the reception she would receive.

The door jerked open.

The business end of a forty-five-caliber automatic leveled on her forehead. She cocked her head, so she could be seen around the barrel.

"Val, what are you doing here?" Smithson Young lowered the weapon and glowered at her. Valkyrie took in all of the man and enjoyed the view. Standing at his door in nothing but boxers, his impressive six-foot-seven-inch frame blocked any view of the apartment behind him. His heavy, bulky muscles were mountains on a vista she could admire forever. Her view of him left little to the imagination. He was indeed spectacular.

She smiled and looked at her watch. "I've come to take you on an adventure. We have five minutes. You should get dressed."

Smith didn't say a word as he crossed his arms, the gun still very much grasped in his hand. "At this time of night? What are you up to?"

She flipped her hair over her shoulder and lifted a perfectly manicured hand. "It's morning. We're going somewhere." She motioned between them. "Go put on some clothes, please. Business casual."

"Why?" The big man continued to stare at her.

She smiled at him. "Because it'll be fun, and I know you don't have anything planned, and neither do I."

Smith didn't say anything for at least thirty seconds. She could practically see the gears and wheels turning in his brain. Finally, he sighed and nodded before turning, and she stepped into his apartment after him, shutting the door. She pumped her fist in the air as he strode back to the bedroom. An unladylike gesture, granted, but the victory was hers. Val waited until she heard him moving around in the bedroom before she went to the freezer, opened the door, and pulled out an old plastic container lined with tinfoil. She opened the top and retrieved his passport, leaving the cash he had stashed in the plastic tub alone. It would be her treat. Putting the container back, she closed the door and positioned herself where she'd been standing when he left.

She leaned against the front door while waiting for him to get ready. Smith's little apartment was not her idea of habitable space. Sparce, no, barren was a better descriptor. There was one recliner that had seen better days. A cement block set on its end acted as a place to hold Smith's television remote. His kitchen consisted of a refrigerator-freezer combo, a hot plate, and a microwave. A weight set and a pull-up bar was his only interior decoration. Depression meet gymnasium was not a good look for any room. Well, maybe a prison yard, but, in her opinion, Smith deserved so much better.

He stepped out into the hall, and she drew a sharp breath. God, he was intoxicating. He wore black slacks, a crisp white button-down, and black leather boots, adding another inch to his already impressive height. She knew that was the suit he'd wear. As far as she knew, he had only one. It was the one he'd worn to Mrs. Henshaw's funeral.

Smith had finger-combed his hair, so it swept back off his forehead. The thick brown hair must have been scared into position because there was no way Val could ever make her mane stay in that style. His suit jacket was in his hand, and he had a five o'clock shadow that was sexy as hell. Smithson Young was a walking, talking poster of the hot bodyguard prototype, but the man didn't know it. Smith had no sense of value about himself that she could detect. He always deferred any compliment or ignored it. At first, she thought the brush-off was a pick-up tactic, but it wasn't. It was just how Smith was. The man genuinely didn't believe he was worthy of any compliment. Smith reached for his shoulder holster, but she stopped him. "No need for weapons today."

Smith stopped and cocked his head as he looked at her. There it was. That resting bitch face told her she'd pushed him about as far as he would go. She hurried to explain. "This is a surprise, and you can't take any weapons with you." She sauntered over to him and brushed some imaginary lint off his shoulder. Since they had lunch after Mrs. Henshaw's funeral, Val had elbowed her way into Smith's life. He was a loner, and so was she. Smith was a Guardian, which meant he was safe. Besides, she'd checked. He'd been vetted. He was someone with whom she could spend time, thank God. With her work for Guardian on pause, she had time on her hands, and Smith had become a ... project. No. Check that. More like an obsession. *Which was kind of stalker-y. Was that a word? Whatever.* Val waited for Smith to make his decision. There was no use trying to rush him, which was something she'd learned right away. He was an immovable object. A mountain. And a delicious-looking mountain at that.

"Just a minute." He moved back to the bedroom. Hopefully to lock up his weapon.

The second time they went out to lunch, she'd appeared on his doorstep just like that morning. It took five minutes to convince him he should eat lunch with her again. They'd spent hours at a small bistro, visiting about everything under the sun. Well, she'd visited, and he'd said enough that she didn't feel too much like a babbling idiot. During that lunch, she'd asked him if he had ever had any trouble with the residents where he lived.

He lifted his eyes to hers and spoke one word. "No."

That precise moment was when Val *knew* she and Smith were compatible. Of course, she'd suspected it for years. The look in his eyes at that moment was one she'd seen every morning in the mirror. For her, that familiar expression began its metamorphosis the day her husband was murdered. Yes, that look was the absolute confidence of knowing no one could hurt you any deeper than you'd already been hurt and the knowledge if they tried, they'd be dead. They held that eye contact for too long. But it seemed neither was willing to break the link. Unfortunately, the waitress severed the gaze, but not the connection. Val had been planning their outing since that day because she'd given Smith access to that utter loneliness inside her, and he'd taken up residency. Now, to let him know. Which could blow up in her face.

"Ready." He grabbed his wallet and hung his sunglasses from the unbuttoned collar of his shirt. She opened the apartment door and waited as he deadbolted all three locks. Smith opened the car door for her, and she slipped into the vehicle. "Next stop, please."

The Guardian driver nodded and pulled out into the street. "Where are we going?" Smith stretched and yawned.

"A surprise." She was taking him away. She'd bought his clothes, arranged the hotels, and scheduled special access to the museums and historical sites that he'd spoken about but had never seen. Over the course of the last three months, she'd realized that Smith was probably one of the most intelligent people she knew. That was a bold statement because Val knew an *Operator*. That wasn't public knowledge, but if Smith and Aspen ever met, the conversation would be amazing.

Smith settled into the back of the car and closed his eyes. She smiled to herself. He trusted her. Either that, or he was exhausted. She placed her hand on his leg. "What time did you go to bed?"

He opened one eye. "About ten minutes before you pounded on my door."

"Sorry. It'll be worth it, though, I promise." She patted his thigh. "Go to sleep. I'll wake you when we get there."

The drive to JFK was quiet except for Smith's steady breathing. Val studied his sleeping profile as they sped through the night. To an extent, the man was a mystery. She knew the basics about how he came to be in Guardian. It didn't take much to get that information. But while Smith appeared aloof and damn abrasive at times, she felt his loneliness. It was there. Hidden, yes, but there, nonetheless. When the Guardian driver pulled up to the departure gate, she woke him. "We're here."

He blinked and sat up, scanning the area as he woke. "An airport."

It was a statement, not a question, but she answered anyway, "Yes. Come on."

She moved to the door when his big hand fell on her shoulder. "What are you up to?"

She turned to face him. *Time to let the cat out of the bag.* "We're going to Europe. I have it all arranged. I want you to see everything. To experience Amsterdam and see the Venice canals you described so vividly to me. I want you to lose yourself in the Louvre, to marvel at the beauty of the Crown Jewels, to sit in awe of Stonehenge and touch history. You know everything about all the wonderful places, but you've never been to them. We have time off work; I have more money than I can spend in two lifetimes, and I want you to have this. Please come with me."

The driver, who'd exited the vehicle, was extracting their luggage from the trunk. "You packed clothes for me?"

"Yes, and I stole your passport out of your freezer." She pulled it out of the pocket of her purse.

He took the blue folder from her. "Do I want to know how you knew where it was?" He nodded to the door, and she smiled. *He's going to come*! That made her insanely happy, which would make Reaper laugh out loud. The assassin liked to tease her. So she would never tell Reaper about their journey. Far be it from her to give her friend ammo to volley in her direction.

She opened the door, stepped out, and waited for him to unfold from the car before hugging him. He patted her back but didn't hug her. That was okay. She had time to work on that. "I may have poked about your kitchen and found it."

"Poked about? Is that what you call searching someone's home these days?" He lifted the handles on three of the four cases the driver sat on the curb.

"Meh, it's all shades of the same color, and your apartment isn't exactly huge." She grabbed the handle of the last bag. "Thank you." She spoke to the driver. The Guardian nodded and headed back to his car.

Val walked beside Smith as she pulled her suitcase behind her and directed their route to the ticket counter to check their bags. After getting through security, she put her arm through his and led him to the lounge where they'd wait for their flight. Smith took everything in, although he wasn't obvious about it. She saw his eyes bounce back and forth, intent and scanning, clearly alert. Another reason she liked him. He was very present in his surroundings. He wasn't one of those men who trudged through life expecting the world to shift to his whims. As the assassin in her would say, Smith assessed every situation, making him an even better travel companion.

"Air travel has changed since I last flew," he mused as they sat down in the lounge. An attendant was with them immediately, and they ordered coffee and pastries.

"When was that?" she asked when the attendant left.

He drew a deep breath and let it out. "After I graduated high school."

"Where did you go?" She turned to face him on the couch they were sharing.

"Home." He shook his head, and his jaw tightened.

"Where's home?" she asked as the attendant arrived with their coffee. Val took the saucer in her hand and leaned back, facing Smith again.

"Wherever I lay my head." He took a sip of his coffee. "Where's home for you?"

Val chuckled. "Touché." Smith was a verbal sparring partner like no other. If he wasn't in the mood to disclose anything about himself, he was a vault without a combination.

"What are you doing here, Val?" He put his coffee cup on the small table and turned to face her.

His jaw ground together, and she sensed the barriers she'd torn down start to go back up again. Damn it. She stopped with her coffee cup halfway to her lips and spoke before she took a sip. "What do you mean?"

SMITH BLINKED AT HER QUESTION. *What did he mean? Wasn't it obvious? Okay, he'd spell it out for her.* "Why are you doing this? Why me? What's your endgame?" He gave a harsh laugh and rubbed his face with his hand. "Val, I'm not a dirty child that you can brush off, dress up, and teach manners, so you can parade him around polite society. I have a past I'm not proud of that has made me the man I am. You're in a losing proposition if you're betting on reforming me." He sighed as the anguish of his past consumed him, lowering his eyes to his shoes and shaking his head. No, he wouldn't allow that to happen. He spoke clearly, but quietly. She needed to hear and understand him. "I won't be used again." Not even by the beautiful woman sitting next to him. He'd learned that lesson the hard way.

She sat her coffee cup down and stared at him. Her blue eyes narrowed a bit. "I'm not trying to change you or use you. I know about your past. About that son of a bitch Simmons and what he did to you."

Smith's head snapped up so hard his neck cracked. Hatred surged to the surface of his consciousness in a tidal wave. *That fucking bastard.* He glanced around and hissed lowly, "What do you know?"

Val's whisper returned just as urgently, "That he made you do what you did. I don't know what he was holding over your head to make you do it. I wasn't told, and I don't care. I've made my judgment about you from my interactions with you. You *don't* scare me, Smithson. You *can't* hurt me. I am dead certain I'd never let you place *me* in a position to be hurt, nor would *I* do that to *you*." She moved closer to him, put her hand on his leg, and whispered, "I work for Guardian. You know that, but you've never asked what I do for them."

Dear God. He swallowed hard. His mind raced, grasping at thoughts that flashed by, chased by others that he couldn't prevent. At least she didn't know what Simmons had used to blackmail him. He'd been able to bury most of those memories and all the evidence—he thought. He never questioned Dixon Simmons when he said he'd deleted the evidence. Perhaps he should have. He rubbed his face with his hands. That woman was of legal age when he had relations with her. Dixon Simmons' father, that bastard, had fabricated documentation showing her to be too damn young. Criminally young. He closed his eyes. He would never, never take advantage of a *child*. That fucker Simmons had backed him into a corner with his morals and kept him there using a video of him having sex with the woman and made-up birth documents.

His stomach rolled as nausea lurched up his

throat. "Simmons ... I never want to talk about that time in my life. Ever." No, he'd never asked what role she played at Guardian. His guess was she was in a high-ranking administrative position. "What you do for Guardian doesn't matter."

She shook her head. "It actually does. I do select jobs for Guardian in much the same way you worked for Simmons."

What in the hell! He jerked back as if she'd slapped him and bit out in a whisper, "No. Guardian doesn't do *that*." He'd murdered people for Simmons. Innocent people who didn't deserve to die.

She cast a gaze around the lounge and leaned in. "Come closer." It took a long minute before he leaned forward. God, she had no idea what he'd done. What he'd been *forced* to do.

She whispered in his ear, "There's an international entity that targets monsters like Simmons, but the demons they go after act on a far grander scale than that bastard ever dreamed of going. There are assets worldwide that hunt people who evade justice, who are responsible for genocide and unimaginable atrocities, and who cause the suffering of multitudes. Smith, I've experienced your blackness. I live in it. I'm not here to change you. I wouldn't do that to anyone."

The attendant stopped by and could obviously feel the tension between them as she dropped off the pastries and didn't offer to refill their coffee. He waited until the waitress was out of earshot, even though they were still whispering so low they could barely hear each other. Alarm bells and warning flags were sending up caution markers right and left. *Why him? What was Val's impetus? Why now? Why the trip? Why the casual meetups for the last few months?* Nothing calculated into a solid answer. "Why are you telling me this?"

She stared at him and cocked her head. "Because you asked me why. You deserve the truth."

"And yet you haven't answered *that* question." He held her gaze and whispered, "Why me? Our so-called *shared* past experiences aside, why me?"

She let her eyes drop to his lips and then lift back to his eyes. "You felt the connection we have. You can't deny it." He stared at her but only nodded. Once. Hell, yes, he felt it, but could it all just be about a sexual attraction? With him? Lord, if life had taught him anything, no one was polite, nice, or kind to him without wanting something. There had to be something more. Some underlying reason a woman as beautiful as Val would pay any attention to him.

She leaned forward. "I'm not playing with you. I don't want to change you. I'm getting to know a man who intrigues me. I'm touring Europe with him. Yes, perhaps I'm looking for an adult relationship for however long that lasts between us. This trip, a season, a year? Who knows. Or perhaps you don't find me attractive. I'm not going to lie, I would be disappointed, but I won't force the relationship if you don't want it. No matter about the attraction, we're both lonely as hell. I can see it in you just as I can see it in myself. We can still travel; more will never happen if it isn't in the cards for us."

Not a single experience in his life allowed him to believe any of her explanations. No. He looked around. Was she setting him up? Or ... God, why hadn't he ... "This is a joke, right? Am I a joke to you? Is all this, the lunches and dinners, a game to you?"

She pulled back a bit. "What? A game? I don't understand."

Smithson turned and looked around the

lounge. "Look at the people in here, then look at me. I'm not like them."

Val blinked at him. "Thank God. I wouldn't waste the time of day on most of the people in this lounge. I don't consider this friendship a game."

Friendship? Yeah, he'd guessed that was what it was. But holy hell ... she couldn't be serious. He raked his hand through his hair, frustrated, but kept his voice low, "I am not someone who should be with a woman who looks like you. I *am* nothing. I *have* nothing."

She leaned forward, putting herself within an inch of his face, and tugged on his shirt. He leaned back to put her in focus. Her blue eyes blazed with anger. He pulled away, but she grabbed his shirt and tugged him back before she whispered, "Bullshit. You're a brilliant man. I've seen that, so listen up, Smithson Young. First, nobody, not a soul in this world, is allowed to tell *me* what kind of man *I* can be attracted to. Second, you aren't a nobody. You're the man who cared for an old woman to pay a debt he didn't really owe. Guardian took you in to look after Mrs. Henshaw because they *knew* you could be redeemed when you'd been screwed over by that fucker Simmons. I think you're sexy, and

I'll be damned if I let anyone tell me othe.

She leaned in and kissed him on the lips.

Too shocked to move, he froze but took in every sensation of her lips against hers, her soft body warm against his chest. She finished and moved back a fraction of an inch. Smith tried one final time, whispering against her lips, "Bad shit follows me. You should run away."

"I don't run. I never have, and I never will." She gasped when his arms circled her and pulled her toward him. God help him; he was going to give in to her. There would be a price, and he might not survive it, but damn it, she was irresistible.

He whispered, "I warned you," before he lowered his head and kissed her.

2

Holding Val was heaven and hell in the same instance. He kept his kiss chaste. She wasn't the type of woman to maul in public. Too soon, he ended the contact, and she sighed. Her warmth against him was something he steadfastly refused to believe could happen. He'd killed people, and still, having her in his arms fucking terrified him. His heart pounded a million miles a minute, and that fear kept him mute. God, he couldn't mess it up. Yet, it was guaranteed to go sideways. It always did.

"I'd tell you to stop thinking about it, to take it as it comes, but one thing I've learned about you is you examine everything in finite detail." She placed her hand on his chest. Val was a tactile person. He'd realized that when he'd first met her. Those lingering touches were her way to communicate; he'd written them off as exactly that and nothing more.

He nodded. The situation, revelation, hell, *upheaval* of his norm would keep his mind spinning. As always, he'd look for the sucker punch. The universe didn't hand out good things to him without taking its pound of flesh in return. "Critical thinking is a self-preservation skill I developed far too late in life."

She smiled at him. "Look before you leap?"

He felt the corner of his lip tick up. Val could make him smile despite himself. "Something like that." More like if you want to live, make sure you know who's pulling the strings and why.

"Well, you're still alive, so you didn't learn the lesson too late." Her soft laugh eased the caution moving through his veins as sure as his blood circulated through his body. He'd sworn to himself that he'd never be placed in a compromised position again. And yet, there he was.

Falling head over heels in lust with Val, the first time he'd seen her at Mrs. Henshaw's apartment all those years ago had taken him by surprise. Guardian had appointed him Mrs. Henshaw's caretaker. The old woman had been adopted by several of Guardian's operatives when her family had basically forgotten she existed. Being her caretaker was a penance and a pleasure, and she became the mother figure he'd never had.

Val visited Mrs. Henshaw regularly, like several others, but he looked forward to her visits and the brief time in her presence. Her beauty, elegant grace, and pure sophistication placed her in a category of women he hadn't associated with in over twenty years. Twenty hard years filled with death and violence. He'd survived in the sewer and associated with rabid animals. He was no longer worthy of holding her or any other lady of her ilk in his arms. He closed his eyes, hoping his life of filth didn't invade Val's world. He'd tried to warn her.

"Oh, I have something for you." She moved away from him and reached into her bag. He recognized the Hermes brand. His mother preferred Hermes. The one Val was digging through probably cost six figures. Another reason he shouldn't be with her.

She pulled out a small pearl inlaid box and opened it. "Here." She placed a small device in his hand.

"This is?" He looked at her and then at the earpiece.

"Communications. I don't know about you, but aircraft noise is not my favorite thing to talk over. We'll be able to talk and hear each other with these, and no one else will be a part of our conversation." She slipped hers into her ear. "Don't worry. We're not being monitored right now."

He cocked his head at her. "Right now?"

She motioned to his ear, and he slipped the piece in. "Guardian can monitor these pieces. Or they could. I'm not sure of their capabilities right now. But they did monitor them before the attack. The bottom line, I'm not currently working. They're not currently listening." The words she spoke were crystal clear and loud in his ear, although she looked down at her purse, seeming to organize the contents. She was barely talking above a whisper.

"So don't talk too loudly, or I'll blow out your eardrum."

She glanced up at him and smiled. "They're regulated for optimum volume. You could scream, and it wouldn't get louder or softer." She placed her hand on his leg. "You won't regret this trip. I promise. We'll have a wonderful time."

Smith covered her hand with his. “Just tell me when you want me to leave.”

“Let’s start the journey before we finish it, shall we?” Val nodded toward the monitors. “Our flight’s up. It’s time to board.”

THE AIRPORT WAS CROWDED, but Smith used his size to keep the press of people away from Val, and she smiled at him when he moved between her and a man who wanted to board before them. The aggressive passenger tapped him on the shoulder but failed to utter a word when Smith turned and glared down at him with a look that would send the minions of hell back to Satan’s nest. Most people were easily intimidated. Knowing which specimen of the human race would be trouble was a skill Smith had developed while surviving on the streets. The blowhard behind them wasn’t a concern.

Smith walked with Val down the gangway and into the aircraft. He had to bend down to enter the plane, and standing straight wasn’t an option as he followed her to the front. At least the compartments, or pods, as Val called them, were spacious enough to extend his legs fully, a luxury he hadn't expected. The last time he'd traveled, first class was nothing but wider seats and a curtain barrier between the people who had and the people who had not. The wall between their pod lowered and exposed Val, sans shoes, curled up in her seat facing him. "Do you have enough room?"

He smiled. "The chair is more comfortable than my recliner at home." Which wasn't a stretch. The recliner, purchased from a second-hand store, served its purpose.

Val smiled at him. "Why don't you have a nicer apartment? I know our employer pays you."

He leaned back in his chair and stared at her for a moment. "I'm not one to spend money on creature comforts." He'd squirreled every penny he could into several stashes. Cash money he could get to and use, so he'd never be in a position to borrow again. Money was what plunged him into the underbelly of New York. He hadn't touched any of his pay since Mrs. Henshaw passed. It was undoubtedly an error, and as soon as Guardian restructured, they'd see their mistake and want the funds back.

She stared at him. "I've been meaning to ask you. Where were you educated?"

He lifted an eyebrow. "You first."

She laughed as one of the cabin crew stopped by to take their preflight drink orders. Val ordered champagne, and he asked for bottled water. When they were alone, Val answered him. "I was born and raised in Minnesota. I went to school there, but our employer gave me my education. Your turn."

"Preston Heights Military Academy. Beyond that, life has been my headmaster." His parents had shipped him off at the age of six, and he spent one month every year at home over the Christmas holiday. He didn't know how much his parents paid to have him at the academy during the off months of summer vacation and during Thanksgiving and Spring breaks. The instructors and staff raised him. Not his parents. During those long, lonely vacation breaks, he'd spend all his time in the library. He could travel in his mind, fight dragons, duel musketeers, travel to the stars or the depths of the oceans, and forget his solitary existence.

"College?" She took a fluted glass of champagne from the tray as the attendant made his way past.

He glanced around the first-class pods.

Everyone was settling in and either wearing headphones or looking at their phones. There wasn't any need to feel self-conscious, but he did. He spoke low, knowing the communications device would amplify his words. "My parents decided I should make my own way in the world. My future had a foundation from a prestigious preparatory school and nothing else."

Val turned, so she faced him straight on. "They turned you out?"

Smith nodded. With one suitcase and fifty dollars. "I bought a bus ticket from Connecticut to New York City. The first mistake I made." There had been so many more. But he was able to use his size to survive. He glanced down at his knuckles. The scars were visible. He'd learned to fight, to steal, to survive. He fought to live, and when he grew strong enough, he hired his skills out and fought for others. For monsters like Simmons.

"I couldn't imagine what it would be like not to have anyone to help. My parents were older, but I had aunts and uncles." She swallowed hard. "I'm so sorry for that young man."

Smith blinked and cocked his head. That was an interesting turn of words. "Not for me, though?"

"For the younger you, yes. He had to be terrified and, in the end, forced into unfathomable positions. For the man I'm looking at now. No." Val reached for her champagne flute.

"Why's that?" He leaned toward her pod.

"Because the man in front of me is resilient, strong, determined, and intelligent. He doesn't need my pity."

A slow smile spread across his face. "I would not welcome your pity."

She smiled back at him. "See. I love being correct." She chuckled, then seriously asked, "Have you spoken to your parents or sisters lately?"

He shook his head. "I have no connection with my sisters. They went to different boarding schools, and we were strangers living in the same house when we were home. I haven't spoken to any of them since I walked out that door almost twenty-one years ago. My parents weren't the most nurturing. I can only assume they did what they thought was best."

"For themselves," Val snipped.

"Probably," Smith agreed. "I wouldn't put them up for parents of the year, but there are far worse out there." He'd read reports and studied the science behind familial bonding and why it did or didn't happen. Still, he didn't understand how his parents thought turning him out would benefit anyone. Rational, logical intelligence, which he knew he had, couldn't connect the dots on his parent's cognitive processes.

Val grumbled something unintelligible, and he tapped his ear. "I'm sorry, I didn't catch that."

"Worse children, too. Like Mrs. Henshaw's kids." Val tipped up her champagne and finished the glass in one go. "I hate those people. I've schemed a million ways of making them pay for abandoning her."

"She was proud of them and what they'd accomplished. She loved them." Smith had sat with her in the evenings, listened to the same stories, and witnessed a mother's connection. It was the first time he understood what unconditional love looked like.

"Well, she was a better person than I am." Val huffed.

Smith reached out and took her hand in his. "I don't believe people can be graded by goodness. People are moldable based on innumerable influences and pressures. Goodness is only one facet of a complex formula."

Val threaded her fingers between his. "How do

you categorize those who are good versus those who are bad?"

He hummed and nodded his head. "I try not to do so. I've been taken advantage of by people I thought were good and helped by those I knew were bad. Good and bad can be mirages. In my experience, a person is a threat, or they're not. Assuming shades of anything beyond that leaves you vulnerable."

Val stared at him for several long seconds. "I am not a threat to you."

He smiled. "I believe you don't think you are. However, this attraction between us makes me vulnerable. Therefore, you are a threat, but you're one I'm willing to engage, and any damage done will be accepted as a consequence of my attraction to you." One thing he knew, there would be payment rendered. He just didn't know what the cost would be.

The cabin crew announced prep for takeoff, and they strapped on their seatbelts. The wall between them was lifted for the taxi and takeoff. Smith closed his eyes and felt the vibration of the aircraft around him. "I don't want you to think of me as a threat." He could hear Val's words but not see her. It was eerie. He smiled, although she couldn't see him.

"I understand, but I cannot change what I see."

"Then I'll be vigilant to mitigate any consequences you may face due to the attraction between us." Val's words vibrated in his ear.

"Are you mocking me?" He chuckled when she groaned.

"No, I was trying to be reassuring," she huffed.

"Thank you." Most people would overlook his opinion or not give a damn. In the short time he'd been in her company after Mrs. Henshaw passed, Val had treated him with respect, friendship, and humor. A heady combination.

3

Val stared at the lifted partition between her and Smithson. His analysis of the relationship, the fact that she'd leave him vulnerable, was probably true. But she needed him to understand she was leaving herself vulnerable, too. Together, they could be stronger. "You're not the only one who'll be vulnerable."

There was a hum of agreement from him. "Then I'll return the pledge. Based on our developing relationship, I'll endeavor to mitigate any vulnerabilities to you."

Val cringed. "That sounds like a transaction. I want us to have fun."

"As do I. And I believe I've been negligent.

Thank you for the surprise trip to Europe. The planning must have been intense."

She laughed. "Do you know how hard it was to get your clothes measurements? I dug through the hamper in your bathroom."

There was silence. "That night about two months ago, when you said your stomach was upset?"

She giggled. "Yes. But I was able to get the measurements I needed."

"And will you tell me how you knew where my passport was located?"

"Oh, that's easy. I was hungry, and you had nothing in your fridge, so I looked in your freezer. Which leads to the question, how do you stay so bulked if you don't have food in your apartment?"

The cabin crew announced they were free to move about the cabin and instructed them to stay belted in when seated. The partition lowered, and Smith reached his hand out. She laid hers in his. His eyes were closed. He had to be exhausted. The hour in the car was the only sleep he'd gotten last night.

"Genetics, I assume, play the majority role. If I'm hungry, I go to the corner bodega. The woman makes fresh meals."

"And you what? Eat breakfast, lunch, and dinner there?"

He shrugged, still not opening his eyes. "It's reasonably priced."

"Smith, do you know *how* to cook?" She squeezed his hand, and he opened one eye.

"Do TV dinners count?"

Her mouth dropped open. "No, they most certainly do not." She shook her head. "We're going to rectify that."

He chuckled. "The best-laid plans ..."

"Oh, don't even try to dampen my optimistic ideas of grandeur." Smith laughed, a full-on, deep laugh that resonated through her like a tympany drum in the orchestra pit, finding her center and making her vibrate. Magical.

"I'll use caution on my hydroponic pessimism." He let that half-smile of his slide out for a moment.

"Be sure that you do." She held his hand as he fell asleep, and as his grip loosened, she stared at his relaxed face. A wisp of his dark brown hair strayed from the swept-back appearance and dangled over his brow.

Val waived off the offer for the first meal service, letting Smith sleep. About two hours outside of Heathrow, she gently woke him. “Dinner will be served soon.”

He opened his eyes, and his warm hazel gaze found her. She smiled at him. “Did you sleep well?”

He sat up and rubbed his neck as the seat retracted back into a lounger instead of a bed. “I did.” Looking around the cabin, he asked, “Quiet trip?”

“Except for your snoring,” Val quipped.

His attention snapped back to her. “I snore?”

She chuckled. “No.”

He rubbed his face. “Okay.” He stood up and stretched, although he had to tip his head, so he didn’t hit the aircraft ceiling. “Be right back.”

Val watched as he moved up the aisle. She saw him stop, stoop over, then rise. He handed something to the man in the pod at the front of the cabin before disappearing behind the bulkhead. “Val, 3D printed plastic guns have the same mechanisms, but plastic, right?” Smith’s words came through her earpiece.

Val sat up straight in her chair, instantly alert. “Yes, and if disassembled, would make it through screening. Where?”

“Front right. A firing pin, I could see a barrel

when I handed it to him. The rest was covered with a magazine. Come up the other aisle. I'm standing by the restrooms."

Val slipped out of her pod and made her way up to the bulkhead, taking her time and making sure she examined every person. A man sat in the front pod with a magazine opened and spread across his lap. He glanced at her and then away when she smiled, his hand moving to cover the periodical. Val glanced across the space and caught the individual Smith had identified staring across the cabin at her—or at the man with the magazine.

She found Smith and stopped out of sight of both men. "There's a second person of concern. Also with a magazine in his lap. When I made eye contact, he warded and covered whatever was under that magazine."

Smith nodded, whispering as she was. The earpieces had been for convenience. They'd become a necessity. "How far out are we from London?"

"About two hours." Val glanced at the cubbies on either side of the bulkhead where the crew for their cabin were visiting. "We need to alert the crew."

"If we're wrong?" He crossed his arms over his chest. "It draws attention to us and has possible ramifications."

Val put her hands on her hips and stared at the ground for a moment. "And if we don't act, the ramifications could be horrendous for the people on this plane and possibly others. Tell me what your gut says."

"I've seen this type of mannerism before. The same tension I've witnessed before a newb robs a convenience store or hired muscle goes up against someone they know will beat them into the ground."

"My gut told me the other was warding, as I said. I've learned to trust my instincts."

Smith nodded. "Security is tight in the flight deck area, isn't it?"

"Improved with locked metal doors since nine-eleven," Val confirmed.

Smith rubbed the back of his neck. "It can't be my imagination. I've disassembled enough weapons to know a firing pin. It was white plastic, sturdy. Not strong enough for multiple shots, I don't think."

"It isn't our imagination," Val corrected. "The last intelligence I received about 3D printed weapons was they were good for one shot. The propulsion will shatter the plastic casing. If the bullets are hard plastic, they aren't getting through that door. If they're real, they somehow smuggled them through security, but still, the weapon will only be able to fire one bullet." Val nodded to the front of the plane where the pilots were secured. "We alert the crew and find out if they have an air marshal on board."

"Guardian?" Smith asked as he moved out of the way so a gentleman could use the restroom he was blocking.

"Only if this goes down. I can't be in the light." She glanced at Smith, who narrowed his eyes and knew he was patching together the information she'd told him earlier with her statement. His intelligence once again visible to anyone willing to see it.

"All right. The conversation with the crew is on me." Smith stood aside as the elderly gentleman departed the restroom. "You've got my six." The words were said as he moved to the small galley where the crew was enjoying a bit of downtime.

Val listened as Smith explained what they believed the situation to be. Mentally, she commended the crew. They flew the information straight to the flight deck, and then the woman plastered a smile on her face and headed back to get the air marshal on the aircraft for the flight.

Val caught movement in her peripheral vision. A shoulder was visible as it peeked just past the wall. Same color material as the shirt the man she'd suspected was wearing. "Smith, target's moving."

Val went flush against the wall and moved to the corner where she knew the man would enter the area. As she moved, she unfastened the silk Hermes scarf from her hair and wrapped it around both hands. She waited for her target to move. As one, the two men rounded the corner. Val looped her scarf over her target's extended arm. She spun under his arm and, using her back as a fulcrum and her target's arm as a lever, dropped to her knees. The target's extended elbow dislocated with a wicked pop.

The dislocation's sound was muted as the echo of a weapon discharging rang in her ears. Her target grabbed at her with his good hand. She pushed up and rammed her head under the man's chin. *Fuck*. That move always hurt. She dropped again, completed a roundhouse sweep knocking her target's feet out from under him, and dropped the fucker. She fell into her ready position only to notice her target's neck twisted at an awkward angle. Dead.

She spun. Smith's back was to her. The gun his target was holding was extended. The male crew member was down on the floor. He'd been shot. Someone from first class ran up her side of the aisle.

"Stop!" she yelled. "Get back." She shoved her silk scarf into the crew member's shirt, plugging the oozing hole in his chest. The injured man pointed at the phone. Val looked at the guy's name tag. "Don't worry, Donnie, I'll alert them," she assured him. Val glanced up in time to watch Smith's grip contort the hijacker's hand as the bones crunched in a dazzling display of sheer strength. His scream ripped through the air, and the gun dropped from the attacker's mangled hand. Smith held the man's neck in his other hand and stared at him, his grip tightening on his throat. "Smith, we need him alive. My target is dead."

She saw the tick on the side of his face for a fraction of a second before he lowered the man to the floor, only to wrench the attacker's arm behind him.

"Freeze! Air marshal!" A man rounded the

corner with his handgun drawn. His gun moved from Val to the injured crew member and then Smith. He leveled his gun on Smith and swept the scene. The air marshal caught sight of the dead body.

"Both assailants are neutralized," Smith spoke calmly. "We need medical attention for one of the cabin crew, and the flight deck needs to be notified of what happened." Smith handed out the orders with aplomb that came from confidence. "Do you have flex-cuffs?"

"This is the one who saw the gun and reported it to us," the female crew member said from behind the air marshal.

Smith held out his hand. "Give them to me, so I can secure these guys. That way, you can get back to your cabin. They might not be alone."

"I can't leave the flight deck area," the air marshal said, still not lowering his weapon or giving Smith flex-cuffs.

"He's Guardian." Val nodded toward Smithson. "Federal agent."

Smith shot her a side-eye glance but didn't hesitate. "I've got the flight deck. See if we have anyone with medical training. Ma'am," he said, turning his attention to the crew member behind him, "please let the flight crew know what's going on."

The air marshal took a few seconds to make his decision, then grabbed a plastic bag from his back pocket and tossed it to Smith. "What type of weapon did they have?"

"These two had 3D printed weapons." Smith pointed to the one beside him and the one by the dead body.

"Did you kill him?" the marshal asked as he lowered his weapon, although his finger was still on the trigger. Val liked his caution. It was how she'd react.

"I did," Smith admitted. "He attacked first. This one got off a shot before I could get to him."

"Can you confirm that?" He looked at Val.

She nodded. "Absolutely. I ducked when I saw him come around the corner. The next thing I knew, the other gun went off. I crawled over to help the injured crew member."

The air marshal looked at Donnie. The man swallowed hard but confirmed what Val had said. "He stopped them," Donnie panted through his pain.

The air marshal nodded and pointed at the female flight attendant. "All right, make a call for medical assistance. I'll be in first class and monitor the forward movement after I recruit some of those military guys flying coach to help." The marshal pointed at Smith. "You get them secured. I'll need a statement, and so will the UK cops. This is going to be a fucking mess. You," he moved his gaze to Val, "as soon as medical gets here, you keep everyone out. This is a crime scene. Don't let anyone up here for any reason."

Val nodded and glanced at the flight attendant. He was pale and getting paler. "You hang on."

Donnie nodded. "Cold."

"Yes, this floor is cold." Val smiled at him. "You'll be okay." She kept her eyes pinned to his. The man had grabbed her hand, and she wasn't sure he knew he still held her. She'd seen death too many times to count. The innocent ones always tore at her. The attendant's wound was nasty. Val had seen injuries like his kill, and unless a trauma doc was on board and willing to take chances, Donnie's minutes were numbered.

Smith zip-tied the man under him and then the dead man. Standard procedure, although Val wasn't sure how Smith knew to do it. According to what she'd dug up on him, he hadn't had any official training with Guardian—or anyone else for that matter.

Smith bent down beside her and opened his hand. “Real bullets, not plastic cased.” She looked at the .40 Shorty as he continued to speak, “Less recoil than the 10mm 140 grain, but just as much stopping power.” Smith shook his head. “But they couldn’t get through that door. Not with two bullets.”

A man in his thirties sprinted into the area with the female crew member behind him. “I’m a doctor.”

Val moved out of the doctor’s way, and Donnie’s grip released as she moved. Val and Smith walked to the side of the small area. There was something she was missing. Two bullets? What did they hope to do with plastic guns that would shatter with one shot? Her eyes moved from her dead target to the man Smith had taken down, and then to Donnie and the doctor. “What would convince the crew to open up? To come out or let them in?” She nodded toward the flight deck.

Smith stood and helped her up. “It would have to be a damn good reason.”

Val grabbed his arm. “An explosive device?”

“Fuck.” Smith moved damn fast for such a big

man. Val flew in the opposite direction. Val entered her target's pod and pulled out his backpack but only found a load of crap inside. Nothing.

"Here," Smith spoke to her, and she ran through the bulkhead to get to his pod.

"Shit. Smith, see if either of them has a remote trigger." Val opened the backpack and stared at the device he'd found. She had no idea what she was looking at, and she'd been through Smoke's Bomb-making 101 class. "Fuck. Smoke, I hope you're available."

"Nothing that could be used as a detonation device. The one who is alive isn't talking either." Smith leaned over her. "I could encourage him."

"Maybe it'll come to that, but first, I need my cell from my purse. Alert the aircrew and the marshal and get everyone to the back of the plane."

"Can you disarm it?"

"I don't even know if it's armed, but I know someone who will."

Smith nodded and grabbed the female flight attendant, urgently talking to the woman as he moved toward their seats. Val looked up at a sharp whistle, and Smith lobbed her phone to her. She caught it and turned it on. "Come on, come on." As soon as the phone powered up, she pushed star thirteen and then pound.

On the second ring, a voice said, “CCS.”

“Sunset Operative Thirteen. I have an urgent situation. I’m on a transcontinental flight, and we have an attempted hijacking. We took out the two men involved, but they have an explosive device. I think.”

“Affirmative. Take a picture of the device and send it while I locate Smoke. Tell the aircrew not to deviate on altitude. It may be rigged to go off when you descend.”

“Fucking hell.” Val waived Smith back to her. “Tell the flight crew not to change altitude. It may be set to go off when they do.”

Smith was on it in a second, and she watched as he briefed the female cabin crew member. To give the woman credit, she didn’t hesitate to head to the phone, and she didn’t ask stupid questions.

Val sent the picture of the wires painted white. Earbuds at the end were haphazardly taped on, and wires ran into the seam of the backpack. Val picked at the hand-sewn seam and opened the fold. Shit. Was that C4? Damn it, she wished like hell she’d picked a later flight. She narrowed her eyes. How did they make it through security? She gently sat the pack down on the seat and looked up again. First class was empty, except for Smith, who was heading her way, the two hijackers, and the doctor with the injured cabin crew member.

"What do you need from me?" Smith stood next to her.

"I need Smoke to answer the damn phone."

"I'm here." Smoke's voice came over the phone, and Val put him on speaker.

"Do we have a picture of the device?"

"Hold on. Let me send it." Val hit send. "It looks like it's wired to a flat piece of explosive. C4, maybe."

"That isn't C4. From the contouring, I'd say it's RX-08-HD. A low-viscosity, injection moldable explosive. I don't see an ignition device, so don't use a cell phone around it."

"Too late," Smith said.

"Who is that?" Smoke asked.

"Smithson Young," Val answered. "We're talking to you on my cell."

"I'm not even going to ask what you two are doing together. I already know." Smoke mumbled.

"What do we need to do?" Smith asked.

"Send me a photo of the wires. I need to see the complete device."

Val snapped several shots, including the earbuds, and sent them.

“Well, that is ingenious.”

“What?” she and Smith said at the same time.

“The earbuds. Take one off, but whatever you do, don’t take off both.” Smoke cautioned them.

Val reached forward and pulled off one earbud. The tape had already been loosened. “A naked wire.” She described what she saw as she pulled it away. “Wait, there’s a small battery, like for a hearing aid, attached to the tip of the wire.”

“All right, that’s the ignition point. To blow the device, the two wires only need to connect to complete the circuit. Don’t let them touch.”

“Understatement of the year right there, Smoke.” Val placed the earbud back on the wire and used the dangling tape to re-secure it.

“CCS here. Patching in Anubis and Fury.”

Val stood up and rolled her eyes, mouthing “Sorry” to Smith.

“Fury online.”

“Anubis online.”

“Sit rep,” Fury demanded.

Val started. “We’re on a transcontinental flight—”

“Who is we?” Fury interrupted her.

"I'm traveling with Smithson Young."

"Who the fuck is that?" Fury demanded.

"I know him and can vouch for him. He's a Guardian," Smoke interjected.

"Clearance level?" Anubis added to the inquisition.

"Not high enough," Smoke said.

"He's fucking getting upgraded. CCS, make that happen. Highest priority. Valkyrie, he's your responsibility until then," Fury spat out the commands.

"I'll take care of it," Smoke said. "Charley and Gabriel have an in with the Office of Personnel Management, and until we get our processors back up to speed, we're depending on them for investigations."

"Do it," Fury commanded.

"Well, yeah, I said I would," Smoke replied in his laid-back way. Val loved the guy. He had a way of defusing tension, even tension from the highest levels.

Val interrupted what was sure to be a conversation between the two management types. "Did you want me to finish the brief, or are we going to debate Smithson's clearance at thirty thousand feet with one dead hijacker, a wounded cabin crew member, and one live, if slightly crushed, hijacker?"

"Crushed? That was you wasn't it, Smith?" Smoke chuckled.

The corner of Smith's mouth ticked up. So did Val's. Fury sighed. "Anubis, get with our European counterparts and brief them on the situation if Air Traffic Control hasn't already done so. Val, you need to disappear."

"I know. We'll make it happen." Val nodded. She was prepared to become a wallflower in the situation. "Smith has been the point on all interaction with the aircrew, and I tagged the broken neck of the first hijacker on him."

Fury grunted. "Good call. We can work with that. What airport are you heading to?"

"Heathrow. At least, that was the plan. Not sure they'll let us in British air space now."

"On it," Anubis said.

"CCS, get them up and follow them."

"Flight number?" the woman asked.

"Eight-eight-three-six," Val replied. "Is CCS fully operational?"

"Seventy-five percent for emergencies. It's only been a few months since my office blew up. We have a lot of work to do," the woman said. "However it isn't needed for this. All flights are broadcast for governmental monitoring of Air Traffic Control. I can hop on the back of any number of programs, and … there you are. Approaching Scotland."

"Val, once you get yourself and Smith out of the clusterfuck this situation put you in, you'll call. We'll need a complete debrief." Fury cleared his throat. "Good job. Fury out."

"Oh, damn, I bet that hurt him." Smoke chuckled.

"He's got a lot on his plate," Anubis said.

"True, we all do. Smith, keep Val out of the public's eye. Video, picture, or television. You copy?" Smoke's words sounded more like an order than a request.

"I understand," Smith acknowledged. "I'll do as you ask, but I don't work for Guardian any longer." He glanced up at Val and shrugged. "My employment ended when Mrs. Henshaw passed."

"According to our records, you're on the payroll," CCS replied.

Smith's eyes dropped to the floor, and he replied, "I assumed that was a mistake."

"No. I knew we'd find a place for you. I made that call," Smoke answered. "Charley and I have your six, man. You sure as hell had ours when we needed it. Now, do us a solid and make sure Val is out of the conversation you have with any law enforcement entity, will you?"

"Need I remind you that I can take care of myself? I am not a fainting flower." Sweet sarcasm dripped from her words.

"Yeah, yeah, but having the big guy watching your six will only make things easier. Smith, that device is neutralized. You explain to whatever police entity boards that plane about the need to keep those wires apart."

"I was here. I understand." Smith looked at her as they felt the plane bank into a turn.

"We're turning," Val said to the phone.

Anubis answered the unspoken question. "You've been cleared for an emergency landing at Heathrow."

"How do you know that?" Smith asked.

There was a laugh at the other end of the line, then Smoke answered, "Smith, if you learn anything about us today, it's that Guardian has connections."

Smith's gaze shifted to the front of the cabin. "It would seem."

Val sighed. "We're going to get ready for landing. I'll call when I can."

She signed off the phone after everyone else did. "I need to go take care of a few things. You okay to handle this?" She waved at the bomb and the bulkhead.

Smith straightened and rolled his shoulders. "I am. You don't need to worry; I won't let you down."

She glanced at the curtained partition to the central part of the plane. "You could never let me down, Smith." She lifted onto her toes and kissed his cheek. "When they ask where I am, I'm in my pod, crying in a huddled heap of nerves. Got it?"

Smith fought the urge to smile. "Not a fainting flower, huh?"

"Keep your earpiece in." She winked at him and hurried to her pod. It was time to become someone else.

4

Smith ensured the backpack was stable before heading to the curtained-off area between first class and the main cabin. He opened the curtain, and when the covey of attendants turned, he motioned to the one who'd been in first class with him and said, "Sabrina." At least, that was the name on her uniform.

She came over immediately, saying, "We've been cleared for an emergency landing, but the captain is waiting to find out if he can descend."

"He can. The explosive has been neutralized. You can tell the air marshal he can resume his duties."

Smith grunted when Sabrina hugged him. "Thank you. You're a true hero."

"Is she hugging you?" Val's voice was tinged with a bit of humor.

"Yeah, I'm not. Thanks for the hug." He patted her on the shoulder, answering Sabrina and Val. "I need to get back in there until the marshal takes control of the situation."

"Of course." She let him go and grabbed the phone as he slipped back into the first-class cabin and went to the front. The doctor was sitting beside Donnie, who was obviously dead. "You okay, doc?"

The doctor lifted his head. "No. Not really. This is senseless." The man waved at the dead hijacker and then Donnie. "What type of madman does this?" The doctor's eyes fell on the bound hijacker. "His hand is swelling. Soon, the blood will be cut off, and he'll have permanent damage."

"Yeah, the way it's crushed, he'll probably have that no matter what." Smith nudged the hijacker. "You want your hand to fall off?"

"Fuck you." the man hissed back.

Smith looked at the doctor. "He's good. I'll help you back to your seat."

The doctor shook his head. "Let me clean up. If I walk back there like this, I'll terrify the entire plane."

Smith sighed. "Hate to tell you this, doc, that button was pushed when we evacuated first class because of the bomb."

"A bomb?" the doctor squeaked.

Smith reassured him, "We determined the triggering device, and it's been neutralized. Go out and grab a pod. Law enforcement will want to talk with you, too."

"Actually, we'll be detaining the entire flight. No one is going to make their connections today." The air marshal walked into the area. Smith was pretty damn sure the guy had been listening to their conversation, but Val hadn't said anything. "My name's Geoff Parker. Air marshal. Good work in here."

"Smithson Young. Guardian." And now, he felt like an imposter. Guardian was a company with integrity and status. He was a nobody who'd survived on the streets.

"Yeah, we checked. My people contacted yours when this first started to validate your credentials. Sorry, I had to be sure." Geoff bent over the dead hijacker. "How did this happen?"

Smith cocked his head at the statement. When they spoke, Guardian didn't say anything about the air marshal checking his credentials. But they were working a crisis. "You dislocated his elbow, swept his feet, and he landed awkwardly, breaking his neck." Val's words filled his ear. *What? Ah, Geoff had asked a question, hadn't he?* Smith repeated her words.

Geoff nodded to the living hijacker. "And this one?"

"He got a shot off before I grabbed his hand and crushed the gun."

"How did bullets get through security?" the doctor mumbled from the floor where he sat beside the deceased cabin crew member.

Geoff shook his head. "Two bullets are easy to miss. They process thousands of bags an hour through security."

How it happened was the question of the day. Only air marshals could carry a weapon with ammunition on board a plane. Smith blinked at the marshal as he kneeled and rolled the hijacker. Geoff sneered at the man. "Amateur." Geoff released his grip, and the man rolled back on his face. A hair-thin thread of logic started to develop. *Who told you there were only two bullets?* Smith moved his stance and put his weight on the balls of his feet as a tingling sense of dread curled around his gut.

Geoff rolled his shoulders and nodded toward the side of the aircraft where the explosives were sitting in a pod. “Right now, the explosives are my concern. I’ll take custody of it.” Geoff stood up and hiked up his jeans. Smith caught a glimpse of the man’s badge and the weapon that had been pointed at him earlier. A weapon that would fire a .40 Shorty. *Son of a bitch. He knew where on the plane the explosives were located.*

Smith dropped his arms to hang loosely at his sides, hoping to appear relaxed, although he was anything but that. “It’s surprising how anyone could get the explosives through security.” He looked at the air marshal and narrowed his eyes. “Of course, an air marshal could get that backpack full of explosives and bullets through without any issues.”

“Shit.” He heard Val’s voice just as Geoff’s eye twitched. It was the only warning Smith had, but it was enough. He lunged for Geoff when the air marshal went for his weapon. Smith caught the weapon and Geoff’s hands in both of his, his superior weight and power pushing the gun down and to the side. Smith lifted his knee and flattened Geoff’s balls and dick into pancakes. The fucker doubled over but kept hold of the gun. Holding the gun with both hands, Smith kneed the bastard repeatedly, landing his blows to the man's gut. The gun dropped to the floor with a thud, and Smith lifted Geoff, drew back his fist, and slammed it forward, sending the man flying.

"What the hell?" The doctor was curled into a ball beside the dead attendant.

"Clear." Smith dropped to the floor and spun the air marshal. He used one of the zip ties Geoff had been kind enough to supply and flopped the man to his stomach, zip-tying his hands together.

"Are you okay?" Val was beside him.

"Yeah." He motioned for her to leave. The doctor didn't need to put two and two together. She slipped back, no longer in view.

"Check his weapon." Val's voice in his ear echoed his thoughts.

He picked up Geoff's weapon and dropped the clip. ".40 Shorties and two bullets are missing." He ejected the one from the chamber. Fucking hell.

The captain made an announcement for everyone to be seated and, if possible, to wear seat-belts. Smith chuffed to himself. The two unconscious men wouldn't be seat belted. It wouldn't hurt them to get jostled around some.

"You got the third hijacker," Val said. "Let's pray that's all there is."

He sighed and drew several deep breaths of air, trying to still the adrenaline coursing through his veins. His heart pounded rapidly. That wasn't his life. He was used to being the one on the wrong side of the law. Granted, he never wanted to be there, but he knew what he'd done. He knew he'd never atone for the evil he'd performed under Simmons' control. The faces of the man and woman he'd killed simply because Simmons' son wouldn't make a choice flashed through his mind. He'd never forget the other faces either. The innocent ones that monster had ordered to be killed. He wiped his brow with his hand and stared at the aftermath strewn around him. He shook his head. "When you take a guy on an adventure, you pull out all the stops, don't you?" Smith whispered as he placed the marshal's weapon and magazine on the galley counter.

"A lady always delivers on her word," Val quipped.

Smith felt the airspeed of the plane change. "We're landing." He turned to the doctor. "Doc, sit down in one of the pods and buckle up. You don't need to be injured on landing." The man nodded and carefully stepped over the air marshal, dropping into a pod about halfway to the main cabin.

As the plane started its descent, Smith cracked his neck and leaned against the galley. His eyes traveled from the dead bodies to the two hijackers that lived. *Get ready, Smithson. The fun is just beginning.*

THERE WAS A MASS OF CONFUSION, anger, worry, and anxiety as the plane taxied to a parking space far from Heathrow's terminal. The passengers at the back of the plane had reached their limit of not knowing what was going on, and the flight attendants had their hands full trying to keep order. The chaos was precisely what Val needed. She'd covered her hair in a hijab, changed her lipstick, used a liner to change the shape of her mouth, and grabbed a long black sweater from one of the pods to wrap around her. Placing her dark sunglasses on, she slipped through the curtained area and into the main cabin. People were standing, grabbing their bags, pushing, and shoving in the typical cattle car economy class drill. She slipped under a man's arm as he grabbed a briefcase out of the overhead and stood behind him. A woman a few feet ahead shoved the man in front of her because the satchel hit her on the head when he pulled it out. An attendant broke away from the entryway and tried to settle the two, but the woman was screaming that she would sue everyone. The man pushed forward, and someone threw a punch. Like mice, people scurried out of the way as best they could. Val followed people as they pressed through the middle seats to the opposite side of the aircraft. She grabbed a leather duffle from under one of the vacated seats and pushed her way into the line. When the door to the main cabin opened, police swarmed the first-class cabin. Several moved to stop the fracas as the occupants on her side were told to leave the plane.

When Val got to the door, she assessed her opportunities. There were a couple of men stringing cordons, making a staging area. The outside of the aircraft was humming with people. Shouts from responders on the ground and rapid hand movements spoke to the emotion and confusion on the ground. An attempted hijack wasn't an everyday occurrence, especially one with a bomb still on board. The priority would be to get people out of the area. Just what Val needed.

Firetrucks circled the aircraft along with several dark sedans, their lights flashing and engines running, just outside the cordon. Val moved among the clutter of people and shed the sweater before tucking her white blouse into her black slacks and tearing off the hijab. With haste, she pulled her hair back into a ponytail. A whisp caught on the device in her ear and popped it out. Val twisted to catch it, but her earpiece dropped to the tarmac. She stooped to the ground to retrieve it just as someone stepped on it.

"Damn it." Val grabbed her passport, cell phone, and cash out of the purse, shoved it all in the pockets of her slacks, and stood up. Her gaze searched the cordon that was being hastily formed around the plane.

Her best bet was a firetruck. They'd be empty, and she needed ... there. She lifted her arms and announced in her best British accent, "Everyone, please move forward. Make way for others exiting the aircraft." She herded the crowd. "Keep moving. We'll have transportation here in a moment." She moved with them, giving orders and directions until she reached the cordon. Val walked up to one of the men helping to set up the containment area and demanded, “What’s the transportation status?”

“I have no idea.” The man glanced at her and wrapped yellow plastic police tape around a cone to contain the skittish crowd emerging from the aircraft.

“Give me your radio. I’ll find out.” Val extended her hand, and the man handed her his radio before rushing to stop a child from darting out from under the cordon tape. “Firetruck, Mummy!” The little boy darted away from the man Val had taken the radio from.

She ducked under the tape, walked to a different fire engine, moved behind it, then jumped into the cab. Glancing around the interior, she smiled. “Bingo.” She pulled a ball cap out from between the seats and grabbed a jacket with security badges.

Val dropped down from the cab wearing the cap and carrying the badges. As the bus arrived, she shepherded people in with another worker before sending him back to the mass of people to cull the crowd for the next bus. “Need a ride back.” She stood at the bottom step of the bus out of everyone’s view and looked up at the driver. She held up the radio that squawked with rapid commands. “Superiors needed a firsthand accounting.”

“Bloody hell, can’t they see we’re trying to sort this mess out?” the driver muttered and put the bus into gear. Val didn’t answer over the engine's roar as the bus shot forward. She exited first and darted to the terminal in the opposite direction of the crowd. She made her way to the door and slid the badge through the card reader, checking her watch for the exact time. A series of clicks later, the light turned green. Quickly, she pulled open the door and took off the hat. After pulling her hair out of the ponytail, she tucked it all under the cap, pushing the bill down to cover as much of her face as possible as she raced up the stairs. She swiped the card again and entered the departure gates. Before the door closed, she dropped the ID inside the secure area. Then Val joined the swarm of people and slipped the cap off, tossing it in a trash bin. She pulled out her passport, knowing she’d clear customs without a problem. The passport would never be used again. She had numerous caches of identity and money scattered worldwide, especially in or around major cities such as London.

At the customs checkpoint, she presented the

scan code of the passport, let the facial rec scan her, and walked out. She turned the corner and merged into the small hall where limo drivers waited for their fares. She hooked left, headed to the public transportation area, and hailed a taxi.

A long hour later, she opened her hotel suite door and rushed inside. Fucking hell, she needed a new earpiece, and she needed to contact Smith. She didn't have any spares and hoped like hell CCS could access the earpiece Smith had in his possession.

She pulled her cell out and dropped it on the bed. Taking a long breath, she let it out and began sweeping her hotel room. It was standard procedure, and breaking it could cost a life. Hers. She examined all outlets, vents, lights, and the room telephone, which she unplugged and placed in the bathroom. She'd seen too many devices hidden in base unit phones to disregard that threat. When the televisions were unplugged, she also moved them into the bathroom. Fucking hell, they needed to make those things lighter. She shut the bathroom door and went into the living room, shutting the bedroom door behind her. One final scan of the thermostat before she grabbed her phone and hit speed dial.

"Authenticate warrior." Anubis' command put her firmly back into her comfort zone.

"Norse," she replied.

"You made it out?"

"Yes. I've swept the room as well as I can without my luggage."

"Last known on Smithson?"

"I left him on the aircraft to deal with the authorities. He was damn good in a bad situation."

"I heard. Do you need any cover?"

"CCS may have to wipe a few moments of footage at Heathrow. Timestamp 16:35 local time. I accessed the international terminal via the tarmac with a fireman's badge and departed customs at 16:52 local time."

"Got it," Anubis acknowledged. "Hold on while I get the others online."

Val dropped onto the bed and flopped back. Shit, where was Smith? That was not what he'd signed up for, and she could only imagine what the hell he was thinking. Damn it.

"The Rose is online."

"CCS online. Securing connections."

"Smoke online."

As participants of the call signed on, Val sat up. "Line is secure."

"We have a wildcard in this situation." Fury's voice grated over the line. "Smithson Young. What does he know?"

"About what?" Valkyrie asked.

"You," Fury said, and the "duh" was heavily implied.

"That I work for Guardian." Which was true. "We've known each other for several years." Which was also true. "I met him when he was Mrs. Henshaw's caretaker. After her funeral, we became closer friends. We were traveling to Europe to do the tourist thing." Which was also true.

"Did you report your movement?" Fury snapped.

"She did," Anubis interjected. "Europe for the next sixty days. Various points. Standard communications check-in."

"Doubting my integrity?" Val questioned her superior.

"No," Fury flatlined his response. "I'm doing my job, so can the indignity. Where is Young?"

"MI5," the woman in CCS responded.

"Not MI6?" Fury asked.

"No, Five won the pissing contest," the woman replied.

"Smithson has my extra earpiece. Mine was

destroyed during my evac." Val closed her eyes, waiting for a tirade of "you broke protocol" comments.

"CCS, can you access?" Fury shot the question.

There was a deep sigh. "I can't. I'm not there yet. Two-way is available, but not monitoring. Not yet."

"Have Ethan help you and get it done ASAP. I don't want to leave an asset hanging."

"We'll try, but I'm not liking the odds," the woman said. Val heard her talking to someone else, then a muttered reply back to her. "We're on it."

"All right. Valkyrie, take us through everything, step by step."

"Yeah, because there's a hell of a lot that happened after we hung up. The air marshal was the one who slipped the hijackers the bullets, and we believe he was the one who got the explosives through security. Smith put it together at the same time I did. We were separated, and he took down the air marshal."

"He's a good man, scary intelligent even though he won't let anyone see it," Smoke said to no one in particular.

"The name of the air marshal?" CCS asked.

"Geoff Parker is the name he gave Smithson," Val relayed.

"On it."

"We need to have someone at MI5 to pick him up. I can't show my face." Val wasn't going to leave him out there. Hell, he didn't have any money. Just his passport. She rolled her eyes at herself. Stupid. Damn it. She should have anticipated emergencies.

"Who do we have in London?" Fury asked.

"Harbinger," Anubis answered.

"Get him up to speed."

"On it."

"I'm at the Corinthia. Room nine-forty-five. We're staying together."

"And if he's followed?"

"Why would he be? He's not a suspect," Val reminded him. "We've validated him, right? There shouldn't be any reason to follow him."

"Always prepare for the unexpected," Smoke reminded her.

"Fine. I'll change appearance until we're clear of this mess." She was a chameleon. Hair color, makeup, height ... They were all changeable qualities.

"Hold up, everyone," an unfamiliar voice interrupted.

"Bengal? What the hell?" Fury snapped.

"Turn on your television. Any news channel. It's the Hague. The Peace Palace has been attacked. A small single-engine aircraft. It had to be packed with explosives. Half a co-located building is gone."

Val's head whipped toward the room where she'd left the televisions. "Holy shit. My televisions are in the bathroom unplugged. What's happening?"

There was silence for a long moment, and she knew everyone was watching the events at the Hague. "Is there an active trial today?" Fury spat out the question.

"Hold on, I'm checking." CCS' clipped reply came quickly.

"Ah, shit. Melvin Komal. He's one bad dude. He was indicted for war crimes and crimes against humanity by the International Criminal Court in the Hague in 2010 but evaded capture until two years ago. He's been in a supermax facility awaiting trial."

"Attack at the weakest security point," Smoke said.

CCS spoke quickly, “Archangel wants an all-call. Standby.”

“I’ll sign out,” Val volunteered.

“No, it looks like these assholes attempted to do what was done to us on nine-eleven. You’re involved.” Fury stopped her from hanging up.

“Dom Ops is on.”

“Alpha is on.”

“Archangel, this is CCS. We’re ready, plus one.”

“Who?”

“Valkyrie. She was involved in stopping a transatlantic hijacking along with Smithson Young.”

There was silence for a moment. “A coordinated strike? Why does that name sound familiar?” The gravelly voice of the head of the entire company came across the connection.

“He was Mrs. Henshaw’s caretaker. And yeah, they could be taking a page out of the history books,” the man who identified himself as Dom Ops said.

“Melvin Komal is on trial at the Hague.”

“That’s what the CIA just briefed me on. Too much going on now on the ground, so we don’t know what his status is, but it sounds like something he or his supporters would do.”

"I'm not familiar with him," Dom Ops said.

"Melvin Komal is the leader of the Universal Resistance Army, known as the URA. It's a guerrilla group that used to operate out of Africa. He's the kingpin who ordered the abduction of children throughout South Africa and, whew ... seven other African nations. The kids are taken to become child soldiers or sold as sex slaves. Over sixty-six thousand children have become child soldiers, and the total is still out on sex slaves. Some estimate three times that amount. He's funded and provided child soldiers to wars he's started that have displaced over two million people. He's a major league slime ball." The woman in CCS rattled off the information.

Val had heard about the guy, but he'd never been targeted. One of the ones who was supposed to be handled by the courts to show the population that civilized society was actively prosecuting the world's monsters.

"Valkyrie, give me a bullet point on your situation." Val gave Archangel a concise briefing about what had happened on the plane.

"All right, I'm inclined to think this was a coordinated event. The timing is too close not to be. I'll brief our counterparts. Where's Young now?"

"MI5. They wanted his statement."

"Valkyrie is in the clear?"

"I've deleted all footage of her from when she entered the terminal to when she left in a taxi," CCS confirmed.

"It's going to drive them crazy and may make her a suspect," Dom Ops interjected.

"You are correct. I'll tell them to stand the hell down. They won't like it, but we've returned the favor when they've had operators in our country." Archangel was silent for a moment before he continued, "What are the ramifications of Young's involvement?"

"An upgrade to his clearance is needed. He's been with us since the Simmons incident. Solid. Steady. He also came to our aid when the Siege took down our headquarters. Helped me get Jewell and Bengal out of CCS after he and I dug out Phoenix and the Operator. He's quality," Smoke spoke rapidly.

"That's where I recognize the name. Do what you need to do. Valkyrie, he's your responsibility until we get his clearance upgraded."

"I already told her that." Fury's voice dripped with sarcasm.

"Good for you," Archangel quipped. "Alpha, we

may have to deploy teams to support the Hague situation. I need you to bring the teams back into the fold. We're half-assing our CCS functions, but we're back, starting now."

"Alpha copies."

"We're three-quarter-assing our CCS functions."

Val smiled at the retort. The woman sounded insulted.

Archangel grunted. "Sorry, you are correct. Everyone clear on what they're doing?"

"Crystal," Fury drawled.

"Archangel out."

"Alpha out."

"Have you contacted Harbinger?" Fury asked.

"I have. He's waiting on my call," Anubis confirmed.

"All right. Val, you keep Young in your sights at all times."

"I plan on it." Boy, did she ever.

"The Rose is out."

"I'll have Harbinger call you if there are problems, Val."

"Cool. CCS, is it possible to get an earpiece sent to me?" She didn't know what the logistics were like right then.

Anubis answered, "I have spare earpieces here for each of you. It'll be a day or two before it gets there. We're still pretty scrambled logistics-wise."

"Thank you."

"Ethan had a great idea. We'll jump into the earpiece via MI5's intranet. If he's there, he should be able to hear us, and we should be able to hear him. It'll only work in the building, though." CCS informed them.

"I'll take that call," Anubis replied. "Val, play change up."

"Roger that." She glanced at the clock. "We'll need our luggage from the flight."

"I can do that. I'll have them delivered. You said room nine-forty-five, right? What alias?" There was typing in the background as the woman asked.

"Yes, that's the correct room number." Val then gave her the name she'd registered under.

"Okay. I'll put the orders into the airline's system. Oh, gotta go. Toodles."

Smoke chuckled. "Val, if you need anything, you call."

"That's my line," Anubis chided the other assassin.

"Figured you'd have your hands full with the response to this shit storm," Smoke said.

"True. If she calls you, send me a brief or voice message."

"Deal," Smoke agreed.

"Well, then, if you'll all excuse me, I need to become someone else." Val ended the call and closed her eyes. "Don't give up on me, Smith."

5

Smith sat in an eight-foot by eight-foot office and waited patiently. That was his forte. Patience. He'd developed the skill of waiting into a fine art. He could see through the window in the door and watched as a huddle of men had a heated discussion in the hallway. By their mannerisms, he knew who was the superior, who was not, and who was continuing the argument when the others obviously disagreed with him. The only thing he didn't know was what organizations they were from. But that information would come in time. Val's earpiece was silent and had been since about five minutes after the plane stopped. That conundrum presented several vectors for him to follow. The earpieces could have a limitation on distance, or because of the construction of the MI5's building, the signal could be blocked. Then again, it could be that Val had cut comms with him. The men stopped arguing, and he lifted his eyes back to the door. A gentleman removed himself from the conversation and opened the door to the room where Smith sat.

"Mr. Young, I'm Abe Clearwater, CIA liaison to the British Security Service."

Smith nodded. He hadn't been asked a question and was damn good at keeping his mouth shut.

"Can you tell me the events as they occurred on the aircraft?"

Smith leaned back. "I've already given my statement." He'd excluded Val's presence except for her helping the downed crew member. The last time he'd seen her, she'd wrapped her hair in a hijab and looked nothing like the woman with whom he'd entered the aircraft.

"Yes, I know, and I realize it's been a long day for you, but if you could tell me exactly what happened again, I'd appreciate it."

The man sat down across from him, and Smith narrowed his eyes. "Why?"

"There are some inconsistencies we need to

clear up." The man leveled his stare at Smith. "Like your relationship with the woman you said assisted you and slipped through our fingers at the airport. The one who aided the crew member that was shot, as your statement indicated."

"There is no relationship." And wasn't that the absolute truth. Damn, he wished Val was in his ear, but he had his orders, didn't he? Keep her out of any inquiry. He leaned back in his chair and shrugged. "I talked her up. She's beautiful."

"Did you get her name?"

"Sarah, I think she said. She didn't offer a last name, and I didn't push for it." Smith leveled a stare at the CIA liaison. "Have you called my handlers?"

The man cleared his throat. "Yes."

"They told you not to detain me, didn't they?" Smith imagined the gruff-voiced man running the show could be somewhat intimidating.

"That is not their prerogative. We have information we need to uncover."

The man pulled at his tie, loosening the collar, as Smith stood up. "But not from me. I gave my statement."

"Where will you be staying?" the CIA agent asked as he stood up. Smith's build dwarfed the agent's six-foot-two-inch medium build and frame.

"I have no idea." Which was God's honest truth. He had his passport, no money, and no idea where Val was if she was still around. Her obligations to Guardian were more important than her interest in him.

A shout echoed down the hallway, and Clearwater spun and opened the door. "What's happening?" He grabbed a man in a suit sprinting down the hall.

"The Hague has been attacked. A small plane with explosives."

Clearwater looked over his shoulder at him. "Not again."

"It could have been coordinated," Smith mused. Actually, it probably was. "If our plane hadn't been diverted for an immediate landing, the timing would have been perfect for a coordinated attack."

"Jesus." Clearwater shook his head. "I have to go. Stay in London." The man bolted out of the room, leaving the door open.

Smith stepped out into the hallway and glanced left and right. He'd come up through the garage and wasn't in a controlled area. He wandered the halls and finally found an arrow indicating a direction he should take. No one gave him a second look as they scurried or gathered around televisions.

"Smithson?" The male voice in his earpiece made him jump.

He rolled his eyes and cracked his neck. Lord, he would never get used to that. "Yes?"

"Where are you?"

"Leaving MI5 if I can find the exit. Everyone is rather busy right now." As several men carrying laptops and tablets darted past him, he stood to the side.

"I can imagine. There'll be someone outside to pick you up, but depending on traffic, there could be a delay."

"Val?"

"Safe and secure. We're taking you to her."

"They're looking for her." He adjusted his jacket as he approached the main doors.

"They always do. She's good at what she does. They won't find her."

Smith didn't respond. If there wasn't a question involved, he rarely spoke out of turn.

"Your ride will find you. Hang loose out front. He's about five minutes away." The voice stopped talking, which was okay with him. Smith scanned the area. There was a view of the Thames River, and across the water, he could make out an area he'd love to visit. He oriented himself. Over there would be the Globe Theater. He'd read Shakespeare and did a deep dive on the man himself. There wasn't much besides the biographical documentation found in birth certificates, baptisms, marriage certificates, and, eventually, wills. Yet the man was a master of language and drama.

A person walked up next to where he was standing. "Damn, Val picked a big one."

Smith tipped his head down enough to see the man beside him. Again, he didn't speak. There was no question to be answered.

"You are Smithson Young?"

"I am," he acknowledged.

"All right. Come with me. I'll get you to where you need to be." Smith looked at his ... retrieval, for lack of a better word. He stood well over six feet tall and was broad through the shoulders.

"Who are you?" He wasn't going anywhere without an explanation, even though the gentleman was privy to Val's name.

"That's your ride," the voice in his ear spoke

again, but it was laced with static and popped like crazy.

Smith cocked his head. "How long are you going to be listening to me?"

The man beside him chuckled. "That earpiece is a godsend and a curse at the same time. Come on, Val's waiting. I believe they're hot-spotting off MI5's internet. We'll be clear of them in about five hundred feet."

"Go with Harbinger. He's a coworker of Val's," the voice spoke again, and that was when Smith placed it. It was the man who was on the call about the explosives.

"Lead the way," he said to his ride.

Harbinger spun on his heel and set off, and Smith followed him to a sedan parked illegally. He went around the car and got into the passenger seat, pushing the seat back as far as it would go to get comfortable. As the man drove, he watched as the buildings and stores strobed by. There was a cosmopolitan feel to the city that all cities had. Still, the age of the buildings and the occasional glance at an opulent statue or stately manor differentiated the city from the others he'd been through. He watched as a double-decker bus turned in front of them. The size wasn't that impressive, but the unique history of the buses, originating in France as horse-drawn buses, was, and Smith longed to have a closer look at the vehicles.

"Here we are." Harbinger made a move to get out of the vehicle.

"I can get to the room by myself." Smith exited the sedan and buttoned his suit jacket, looking up at the hotel.

"I have no doubt about that, my brother, but I was told to deliver you to Val in person, and I'm a rule follower." The man snorted, laughing at a joke to which Smith wasn't privy.

They walked through the lobby and took the lift to the ninth floor. Harbinger directed him to the left, and they walked down the thickly carpeted hall. At room nine-forty-five, the man stopped and knocked.

For some reason, he felt like a wayward child being returned to his parents. The door opened, and Val, who did not look like the woman he got onto the aircraft with, opened the door.

"Hey, blondie, I see you're rocking the brown now." Harbinger opened his arms, and Val leaned in, hugging him.

"Wigs are the best. Thank God I didn't have to

color my hair." She turned to Smith. "Damn it. I'm so sorry."

He shrugged. It wasn't her fault the hijackers chose that flight. Why she was sorry was beyond him. Unless she was sorry for asking him on the vacation. Smith blinked as Val talked with Harbinger. If that were what she meant, he'd figure out a way to get back to the States. It would be a big hit on his savings, but flying economy would help.

"I'm out of your hair. Brown or blonde." Harbinger extended his hand. "Nice to meet you, Smith. What you did for Mrs. Henshaw was a good thing, man."

Smith slowly extended his hand and shook the man's hand. He felt he should say something in acknowledgment but quashed the idea when the guy turned and headed back to the lift.

"Come in." Val opened the door wider and stepped back. His gaze swept over her as he walked in. The short brown hair and changes she'd made to her makeup made her look entirely different. She was even wearing contacts, turning her blue eyes brown. He stopped and looked at her tennis shoes. "You're taller."

"About three inches with the lifts I have on,"

she acknowledged as she shut the door behind him and put her hand on his back. "I'm sorry for the complications of the trip, but not for asking you to come with me."

He turned to look at her as she smiled up at him. "They're looking for you."

"They can look all they like. I'm quite good at my job." She motioned for him to go into the suite. "I bet you're exhausted and hungry."

He stopped. "The Hague was attacked. The small plane would have struck about the same time we would have been cleared for landing. By the time the alarm sounded, both aircraft could have crashed."

She nodded. "That's the theory our superiors are working with, but until they get facts, we're on hold."

"Hold?" he repeated.

"Yes. Teams are being recalled, and Guardian will work this case. It has international ramifications. Guardian is an international player, whether or not we're recovering from a TKO."

"What was the endgame?" Smith took off his suit jacket when Val motioned for it.

"Well, someone was being tried at the Peace Palace."

"Yes, Melvin Komal. I've been following the case." The man was a first-class bastard, and although the war crimes tribunal was dysfunctional, Smith was happy to see the man come to justice. Some of the allegations in the media were sickening. Children were his primary victims. Icy hatred washed through Smith. Hurting kids was where he drew the line. Children were innocent, and no one had the right to strip that from them. *No one.*

"Right. I don't know if they were trying to kill Komal ... or had other plans. Maybe Komal wasn't the target. I haven't heard anything more."

"Speaking of hearing." Smith tipped his head and used his fingernail to indicate the small device. "You in my head I can deal with, the other? No thanks."

"Oh, they got it to work? Thanks to someone's size fifteen shoe, my earpiece is now tarmac fodder." She rolled her eyes. "They'll send me a new one. Do you want to take a shower? I'll call down for room service. I'm starving." She reached for the menu. "Steak?"

Smith blinked at her, then looked around the suite. "Clothes?"

"They'll be delivered. There are bathrobes in the closet."

"Where did you get this?" He motioned with his hand, indicating her wig and clothes.

She smiled at him and sashayed toward him. "Anything will be hand delivered if you have enough money. I do, but I don't think we can buy off the rack for you."

He snorted. His minimal wardrobe was specially ordered from big and tall catalogs. Mrs. Henshaw had hand-tailored the suit he currently wore. He missed that woman. She was more of a mother to him than his own had ever been.

"Bathroom's through there. Oh, could you bring the televisions out before you shower?"

He stopped short and turned toward her. "Why are the televisions in the bathroom?"

"They're smart TVs that can be used to watch and listen to people if the right computer hacker is working the keyboard. I didn't have my scanner, so I needed to be sure my conversation with Guardian wasn't monitored."

"Scanner?"

"Yep. It looks like a lady's shaver, pink case and all. I checked it in my bags." Val lifted the menu again. "Steak?"

He blinked as he digested the information she'd just delivered. She looked at him expectantly, and he confirmed, "Yes. Steak."

She picked up the phone as he went into the bathroom. He'd never spent the money to have a smart TV, and now, he was glad he hadn't. The used television he got from the pawn shop worked for him. He moved the flat-screen televisions, which weren't heavy at all, placing them back where the cabling was located in the bedroom and the living room before turning on the shower and finding the largest robe the hotel had provided. He looked at the white cotton and lifted an eyebrow. There was no way it would fit him. He slid one arm in and then the other. The robe cinched his arms back at the elbows. He couldn't even shrug it onto his biceps, let alone his shoulders. Regardless, he still ached for a shower. He'd wear his t-shirt and slacks again. He took off his clothes and laid them neatly over a bar beside the side of the shower. What he needed was the white noise of the fall of water to allow him to think.

6

Val put the phone in its cradle and sat on the large leather couch. The sound of water falling in the bathroom gave her immense satisfaction. Thank God Smith had decided to stay. She'd have booked him the first flight back to New York if he'd wanted to leave. Hell, she should probably still offer him the opportunity. God only knew what would come of the situation in the Hague. Although she hadn't been called in to help with operations, she knew the others had, on occasion, helped with a team's mission. She knew why she hadn't been asked to help, and it didn't bother her. Her expertise was more finesse than banging down doors, although she could take down a man the size of Smith if she had to.

Her cell phone vibrated on the arm of the couch, and Harbinger's number flashed. She answered it on the second ring. "Did you forget something?"

"No. I've done some surveillance on the hotel. It doesn't look like he was followed. Is he registered as a guest?"

"No. Do you think I'm an idiot?"

"Well, you are a natural blonde." Harbinger laughed.

"Ass. Thanks for the all-clear." She smiled as she talked on the phone.

"You'd do it for me."

"True. Why are you in London?"

"I like the weather." Harbinger laughed again.

"Nobody likes the weather in London." She shook her head. "Not my business, I get it."

"Hey, Val, that guy Smith. He's pretty intense. You sure you're not messing with fire?" Harbinger's brotherly side came out big time with those words.

"I like to play with fire. Phoenix isn't the only one allowed to do so." She wouldn't let Harbinger know what she was up to any more than he would tell her what he was doing. It was best to keep everyone at arm's length.

"He took good care of Mrs. Henshaw, Val. Don't use him and throw him away."

She stilled at his words. "Ouch." The whisper conveyed more than just the word.

"You know I love you, Val. This guy has paid for his past mistakes."

Val listened to the fall of the water. "He's different, H. He reminds me of someone I used to know."

There was no sound except for the sound of water for a long minute. "Your husband is gone. You won't be able to find him again." H's words were soft.

"I know. I'm not trying to do that." She got why H was warning her not to hurt Smith. She had a tendency to disappear when emotions became involved. No one was allowed to get close, yet Smith knew more about her than anyone. It was different. She'd opened the gates and found a safe place to play for a while. She'd already explained that to Smith. He could leave with no strings, no heartache, no harm, no foul. When it was done, it was done. No one would get hurt except her. Smith was special. She didn't lie on that count.

"Be good to yourself and stay safe," H finally said.

"Whatever it takes, my sweet friend."

"As long as it takes, beautiful." H disconnected, and she put the phone down. It *would* be different. She knew it would. It had to be.

A knock on the door came about three minutes later, and Val made her way to the door and checked the peephole. "Yes?"

A bellman smiled. "Ms. Baxter? I have your and Mr. Baxter's luggage. It was delivered from British Airway, ma'am."

Thank goodness. She used the wide lens of the peephole to make sure no one else was in the hall and opened the door. One man was nothing to handle. Two or more took work, and she was too damn tired. The bellman brought the luggage in, and she tipped him from the stack of pound notes she'd placed by the door for that exact reason. Once he left, she moved the suitcases into the bedroom. The water turned off, and she knocked on the bathroom door. "Suitcases are here. Let me check the room and the bags for any tags or bugs; then, the bedroom will be yours."

"Sounds good." The deep bass of Smith's voice filtered through the closed door. She opened her case and fished through the packing cube where she'd placed her sweeping device. Grasping it, she pulled the unit in half and snapped it together the way it belonged. The signal immediately jumped to green, and she carefully inspected each case and the bedroom, including the television.

"All good. I'm closing the door behind me." She'd give the man his privacy.

With care, she examined the rest of the suite. As she'd hoped, there were no electronics in the room, which was a relief. She put the small shaver back into its case and placed it by the television. Then she hooked the cable up and flicked the TV on. It wasn't hard to find coverage of the Hague explosion. All the comments were just speculation as the talking heads recapped what was already beaten to death and then pontificated on what little they knew while expounding on grandiose ideas of why it happened and who might have been responsible. As if there weren't enough problems without journalists lighting a fire of suspicion and conspiracy theories.

The door to the bedroom opened, and Val almost swallowed her tongue. Smith wore a pair of jeans and a sweater. My god, they formed to his body like a glove and showed off his muscles and build. "Thank you for the clothes. There's more than I need."

"You're welcome, and I disagree. You only have the basics." She changed the subject. "Have you seen any of this yet?" She waved at the television.

He turned and crossed his arms, immediately tuned into the coverage. Every now and then, his eyes narrowed, or his cheek twitched, but other than that, he was motionless until the segment broke for commercial. "Too few facts, too much speculation," he said, dropping down on the couch opposite her.

"That's what drives the ratings. Speculation." She muted the television and turned toward him. "I know it's not our position to know, but that air marshal really surprised me. How did he do it?"

Smith shook his head. "A friend doing a favor for someone running late? Who knows. It could be there are others at JFK involved." Smith turned to look at her. "I would have walked past you on the street and not known it was you."

"That's the idea. You need an exit strategy when you do what I do; a hint of confusion works wonders. Sometimes only a second's hesitation will suffice. Confusion is always good. Confusion and emotion are the best." She'd use anything she could to escape situations her unique talent got her into.

Smith nodded. "Why the Hague?"

"Komal?" She shrugged.

"Following that logic, if he were to escape custody, where would he go?" Smith crossed his arms again and stared at his feet. The silk socks she'd purchased him moved rhythmically. She'd noticed he bounced his foot whenever he was thinking.

"A country without extradition?"

"Yes."

A knock at the door jolted both of them. "That would be dinner."

"I'd feel more comfortable having a weapon," Smith said as he stood and headed to the door.

"I have a way to get some, but we'll need to make a road trip to get it." A place about forty-five minutes to the north of London was where she'd rented a small cottage. It was her safe house in the country. Miles from anyone and stocked to the gills with everything she'd ever need.

"Tomorrow," Smith said before looking through the peephole. His body was canted to one side. A move only people who were used to being shot at used. He opened the door, and two servers rolled in carts of silver-domed plates. They placed a tablecloth on the small bistro table and unloaded the carts. Val had ordered a bottle of wine for herself and a bottle of Scotch for Smithson. It was his drink of choice if he drank. Val followed the men to the door and grabbed some money from the table, tipping each. Smith shut and locked the door behind the men.

"Let's have a drink." Val went to the small mini-bar and grabbed the wine opener.

Smith picked up the bottle of Scotch. "Rather expensive." The Glenmorangie single malt scotch was the best the hotel had in stock.

"We deserve this tonight." She lifted her bottle of Chardonnay.

He sat down his bottle and extended his hand. "I'll open that for you." Taking the bottle from her, he unwrapped the foil from the cap, then expertly uncorked the bottle and poured her a glass before pouring himself a scotch and adding one small chip of ice to the tumbler. She knew it helped the liquor bloom but wondered how Smith knew. Then again, with the man's intelligence, it wasn't surprising.

She lifted the cloches over the food until she found the plate of appetizers. Placing the dish in front of him, she sat beside him and leaned over to grab a small cracker with a delicious crab spread. He popped one of the crackers into his mouth before taking a sip of his scotch. Then he closed his eyes and sighed deeply. “This has been a heck of a day.” He looked over at her. “I told you bad things follow me.”

Val blinked and laughed. “There is no way that what happened today was caused by either of us. If anything, those people are damn fortunate we were on the aircraft. So I’d say good things followed you today.”

Smith’s jaw tightened for a moment before he spoke. “I guess it’s all a matter of perspective.”

She stared at him, regretting not making time to get to know him sooner. Work and, well, her fear of falling for someone again had held her back. But no longer. She smiled at him. “It’s all about perspective, and today, yours isn’t valid.” She lifted her glass toward him. “To Smithson Young, my protector, the most intelligent man I know, and the reason we’re sitting here having a drink instead of filling a coffin.”

He stared at her for a moment, his dark eyes traveling over her before his lip twitched upward, and he said, “To my friend Val, the voice in my ear and the spontaneity and vivaciousness that has made the last few months ... interesting."

Val laughed as he lifted his tumbler to touch her wine glass. She took a sip of the wine and leaned back against the couch. She wouldn't let the night linger at "friend" if she could encourage a more physical realm. "So, have I made your life interesting in a good or bad way?"

Smithson shifted, so he was facing her. "Good for me. Bad for you." He reached over and touched the ends of a lock of hair from her wig. "This isn't you. You should take all this off. You don't need makeup. No one should come here tonight." He leaned forward and placed a tentative kiss on her lips.

She opened her eyes slowly and stared into his. He was right. There shouldn't be any more interruptions. Most men didn't care what she looked like as long as she was available. Smith was the first to ask her to be herself with him. Well, the first since her husband. But that was a different chapter of another story altogether, wasn't it? "Me without makeup isn't a pleasant sight," she whispered.

He dropped another kiss on her lips and spoke

softly as they separated. “Indulge me.” He leaned back and stared at her. “Please.”

Oh, hell, there was desire *and* heat in that look. She shivered, making sure he saw the reaction he drew from her. “I’ll be back.” She stood and grabbed her glass of wine. “Don’t go anywhere.”

Smith raked her body with his eyes. “I’m afraid it’s too late for that.”

HE WATCHED her go into the bedroom, and when she disappeared, he threw back the rest of his Scotch and stopped breathing as it burned down his throat. Liquid courage was what a few of his low-brow acquaintances on the streets of New York had called it.

He stood and made his way to the liquor cart again, filling his tumbler. As he stared at the amber liquid, he tried to come to terms with what he thought would happen that night. He drew a deep breath and rolled his shoulders. His experience with sex ended years ago when Simmons presented that falsified video and birth certificate to him. He closed his eyes for a moment. He’d been celibate for years. Not out of some higher calling but out of self-preservation. Val had been the only woman to pursue him, and he had no idea why. She claimed the interest in him wasn't a game. He'd never known her to lie, but then again, they weren't social until Mrs. Henshaw's funeral.

He heard the shower turn on and took a sip of his drink. He was a fool. Any man in his position would take what was offered. His hesitancy wasn't because of a lack of attraction. Val's beauty was world-class, so her attraction to him was confusing. Smith glanced at the mirror and took stock of what he saw. At best, he was average looking, and that was stretching it. He was big-boned with a sharp jaw, thick muscles, and dark hair. The clothes she purchased didn't hang loosely like the clothes he bought. He liked how they fit, but he shouldn't get used to expensive things.

Smith knew exactly who and what he was. He was an enforcer. He knew how to fight, how to follow orders, and how to clean up the messes of his bosses. He knew the underbelly of New York like Val knew the inside of a Hermes boutique. No, he wasn't the type of man to be her companion or to take her to the opera or theater, although he'd love to go. His escorting her would be caustic for her. He couldn't hide in public, and the looks he received when he walked down the streets of New York told him that people either feared him or had nothing but disdain for him. He'd grown less concerned about both as the years had gone by, but Val's association with him could affect her status, which was something he didn't want to happen.

Smith took another sip of his drink. His mind was made up. Tonight, he'd spend the night with Val. A single night in heaven's arms. Tomorrow, he'd return to the hell he knew and live out the rest of his life. Guardian didn't need him, and he could find work. He'd always survived. He always would. There was continuous work for enforcers.

The shower turned off, and he took another sip of his drink. Nothing like the rotgut he bought at the corner market a few times a year. He didn't drink much. A man in his position didn't have that privilege. He needed to be aware of his surroundings at all times. When caring for Mrs. Henshaw, he'd needed to be available for her night and day. Alcohol, while a nice diversion from life, wasn't a huge player for him.

When he heard her padding across the floor, he turned toward her. Sweet heavens, the woman took his breath away. The wig was off, and her blue eyes again met his gaze. She had no makeup on, and she didn't need any. Her full lips tipped at the corners. "I told you."

"You're beautiful." The words escaped in a breath of honesty.

She moved, and the silk robe flowed around her body, teasing what was under the soft fabric. The tantalization worked, his body roared to life, and the fire at the base of his spine ignited, sending lightning bolts of sexual awakening through his nerves. She stopped and poured herself a glass of wine before moving toward him.

Val moved into his personal space. The erotic scent of her soap and the knowledge she had nothing on under the robe caused his hand to tremble. He gripped the tumbler tighter. The woman filled in every dream of the perfect lover he'd ever had. She was mesmerizing.

"Are you hungry?" She purred the words.

"Famished," he admitted. It was the truth, and God help him; he wanted to bury himself inside her. He slid his hand through her hair at the base of her neck. "It's been years." His voice rumbled, and he didn't try to hide the truth from her.

Her eyes widened a bit. "Years? Nobody?"

She ran her hands up his arms, and his body

jumped under her touch. "No. No one." He dropped his lips to hers and pulled her against his chest. She licked at his lips, and he let her in, savoring the sweet taste of her. *So addictive, so enchanting.*

Val wrapped her arms around his neck, and he pulled her against his body. She swiveled her hips, and out of pure animal instinct, Smith's hips ground against her as he lowered a hand to move her against him again.

They danced, swaying in an erotic build of sexual need. Holding each other, grinding against each other while kissing and touching. Val broke the kiss, and he stared at her. Her lips were red and shiny from their kisses. Her pupils were wide, and her cheeks presented a rose hue. "Come with me." She grabbed his hand and backed away a step. Smith heard the words, but his feet failed to move. She tugged again. "Please."

He made himself move. His cock straining under the tight denim material. Moving was the last thing he wanted to do and the most urgent thing he could think of at the moment. She walked backward, keeping her eyes locked with his and, God help him, he followed her. He would have followed her to the bowels of hell. Instead, she led him to the bedroom. Once inside, she untied the robe, letting it slither to the floor.

Smith's heart stopped beating. He'd died and gone to heaven. The woman before him was the most beautiful thing he'd ever seen. Her pert breasts were tipped with rose color buds. He let his eyes travel down her body and back up. No one, no model or pinup he'd ever seen, could rival her beauty. She walked backward and sat down on the bed. "I want to see you."

And just like that, the spell broke. She couldn't want to see him. He was nothing. She sat up, her legs curling to the side. "I saw what just happened, Smith. Remember, no one tells me to whom I'm attracted. I want you. I want to be with you. Take off your clothes, and let me see you."

He kept his eyes on hers as he pulled off his sweater, tossing it to the floor. She smiled. "God, yes. More."

Smith unfastened and unzipped his jeans. His boxers came off as he pushed the denim down his legs. He toed off the socks when he stepped out of the jeans. His cock jutted out in front of him. He reached down and stroked himself. Pre-come tipped the end. He thumbed the moisture and used it to stroke down his shaft.

She rose to her knees and moved to the end of the bed. Placing her hand over his as he stroked, she looked up at him as she lowered her mouth to his shaft. He barked a surprised sound as her lips covered his cockhead and closed his eyes, his head dropping back as his hands found her hair. His entire body shook as her tongue circled his shaft, and she lowered. Her tongue would kill him and, damn it, he'd die happy.

She lifted off him. "So damn big."

He grunted something when she took him in her mouth again. He wasn't going to last. The fact he didn't pop off the second she touched him was surprising, but he felt that pooling intensifying as she worked his cock. He gripped her hair tighter, slamming his eyelids shut. "I'm going to ... you need to stop."

Val hummed around his cock, and he exploded. His hips moved forward even though he didn't want to hurt her. He heard her gag. He couldn't stop as his balls emptied. Val stayed with him until he was done. She licked around his cock and kissed the crown before she leaned back. "My turn." She moved back on the bed and crooked a finger at him, opening her legs so he could see her core.

He dove between her legs and moved his shoulders under her legs, opening her like a flower and drawing in the clean, fresh scent of her need. Smith feasted on her and took her subtle direction, wanting to make her feel how he'd felt minutes ago. Her hips lifted in a rhythmic pulse. He entered her with one finger as his mouth worked her tiny nub. He crooked his finger against the pulse of her hips, and she gasped. "Yes."

He felt her legs shaking, and then she arched, pushing against his mouth. The clenching of her core against his finger and her long satisfied groan told him when to slow down. When she shivered and touched his cheek, he stopped and kissed the inside of one thigh and then the other.

She rolled and looked at him when he lay down beside her. She smiled at him, and Smith could see the emotion mirrored in her eyes. "You're beautiful." He pushed her hair back from her face, noting a soft spray of light freckles over her nose.

She lifted onto her elbow. "I wasn't. Guardian gave me this face."

Smith stared at her. "What you have on the outside is beautiful, true, but it's your heart I was talking about."

She snorted and shook her head. "I'm not. Not in the line of work I do."

He shoved the pillow under his head before responding. "Why do you work for Guardian?"

Val shrugged and looked down. "At first, it was a way to escape what I'd done. Now … Well, I've seen the monsters we hunt. I've witnessed what they do to the people of this world. Their humanity doesn't exist. Greed, lust, money, and power are all they know or understand. If I can make the world a safer place by using my talents, I will."

Smith nodded and asked, "Why did you visit Mrs. Henshaw?"

"Because she was a sweet old lady screwed over by her family." Val frowned. "Speaking of which, I need to pay them a visit."

Smith chuckled. "No need on that account."

Val looked up at him. "Why? What did you do?"

He shrugged. Val moved over him and placed her hands on his chest. "What did you do?"

"Nothing that any law-abiding citizen wouldn't do," he admitted.

She pounced on top of him, straddling him.

"Tell me, or I'll tickle you." Smith immediately grabbed both of her hands in one of his.

"Uh-Oh! Someone is ticklish." She squirmed a bit playfully, trying to get away, but he rolled her and pinned her under him before releasing her hands.

"No tickling."

"Fine, then tell me what you did."

"I recognized one of the suits at her funeral. He moved in the same circles as a former employer who didn't operate on the legal side of things. So I assumed her children weren't either. I did some digging. Her children own a distribution and warehousing facility." He shrugged. "It's a front. I saw drug shipments arrive, and there were nighttime deposits of stolen goods in one of the warehouses. I called in an anonymous tip to the feds. I assumed they had the local cops on the payroll."

"When did you do that?"

He narrowed his eyes. "The night you came to pick me up for this trip. It seems longer, but it was last night, wasn't it?"

"Oh, we need to ask CCS to monitor that for us. Everyone loved Mrs. Henshaw." She reached up and trailed her fingers along his lips. "You have the most wonderful soul."

"As do you. Beautiful." He lowered to kiss her and melted when she sighed into his kiss. With the urgency of their mutual gratification out of the way, Smith allowed himself the time to explore every nuance of her body. He wanted to remember every detail, to ingrain each sensation into his mind, so years from now, he could remember the night he'd made love to an angel.

Val wasn't like the other women he'd bedded. She touched, kissed, and moved under him, a part of the physical act, not just available for him to use. He lifted her leg and centered his hard cock at her core. He froze. "I don't have any condoms."

"We don't need them. We're covered. Go slow. You're big."

He nodded and dropped for a kiss as he carefully entered and retreated. Her heat and body gripped him, enveloping him as he slowly worked his shaft into her. She wrapped her ankles around his waist and arched, and he slipped in. Her fingernails dug into his back. "So full. So good."

She moved her hips in a small figure eight, and he groaned. "Fuck." She *was* going to kill him. Death by sex. There were worse ways to go. He withdrew to the tip of his shaft and slowly slid back in. They both shivered when he hilted.

"Make me yours." She kissed him and squeezed her legs, pushing the small of his back deeper.

"I don't want to hurt you." He'd been accused of being too big and too rough.

"You couldn't. I want you faster and harder. Don't stop until we both come." Val arched under him again.

Smith lifted to his knees and grabbed under her legs, bending her back. His hips found a rhythm as he snapped forward and then eased out until just his cockhead remained inside her. Val's body jolted under him as he hilted, and he watched as a flush of rose color built. Her hard-as-pebble rose-colored nipples danced as his body moved. He was so close to finishing that he dropped his hand to her clit and used his thumb to …

"God!" Val stiffened under him, and he crashed over the edge. Red and white splotches formed behind his eyes, and somehow, he'd dropped to his hands over her. He couldn't have explained how he supported himself, but somehow, his locked joints managed the feat.

He carefully dropped to his side, and Val tucked up under his chin. His arms circled her, and he stroked her hair. He'd never had a moment as perfect as that.

They both jolted at a vibration from the living area. "What is that?" he asked.

"My cell," she groaned. "I have to answer."

"I'll get it." Smith rolled off the bed and took a second to gain his balance before making his way out to the front room.

7

Val was almost glad for the interruption because she needed a moment to figure out how in the hell sex with Smithson Young was the best sex she'd had in ... Well, she couldn't remember. She usually didn't climax. She faked it, like most other women. Rarely had anyone made her orgasm once, let alone twice in a night. So maybe his skills weren't an anomaly.

Smith handed her the phone as he slid back into bed, and she answered it. "Sunset Operative Thirteen." Val knew Smith could hear, but since he was getting an updated clearance, she wouldn't censor what was happening now that they were done with the mission.

"Standby."

"Smithson is with me." It was protocol to identify those within hearing range.

"Copy. Standby," the man said again. Val didn't know how many people were operating in CCS. Usually, she worked through the Operators, but they were at a unique time in the agency's history.

She yawned quietly and pulled the Egyptian cotton sheets over her and Smith. Something about lying naked while talking to superiors didn't seem appropriate.

Smith's fingers floated through her hair, and she closed her eyes. It felt good just to lounge with him. She hadn't felt this relaxed since ... Her eyes popped open.

"What?"

She looked up at Smith. "What, what?"

"You jumped?"

"Did I? I didn't mean to." Which was the truth.

"Archangel online," a voice came over the line.

"Dom Ops online."

"The Rose is online."

"Alpha online."

"The Annex is online."

"CCS is online with Sunset Operative Thirteen and Smithson Young. The line is secure."

"Thank you, Ethan. Where's Jewell?"

"Currently trying to debug a wiring harness that isn't working." Val recognized Bengal's voice immediately.

"Copy. All right, this is the status as we know it." Archangel's gravelly voice was immediately identifiable. "The area around the Peace Palace was the target of both planes. The hijacker who was killed had terminal cancer and was going to take the plane to the ground. The other two were going to parachute out. The parachutes were stowed where the crew kept blankets, pillows, and assorted items for the first-class travelers."

"How did we learn that?" Anubis asked.

The man who identified himself as Dom Ops answered. "The CIA has its methods. Let's just say the air marshal doesn't like water."

Val tipped her head back to look at Smiths, who shrugged, completely nonplussed by the disclosure.

"Why?" Val asked the question.

"We were right. This was a strike organized by Komal's people. There were teams on the ground. The court was swarmed, and Komal was freed."

Val knew what that meant. He would be targeted if he wasn't already.

"Any intelligence as to where he fled?" Smoke asked.

"A non-extradition country for sure," Alpha said. Val liked that guy. She'd heard him on calls before.

"The list of closest non-extradition countries?" Archangel asked.

"Hold on." Val heard typing.

"Russia, Morocco, Moldovia, UAE, Qatar, Bahrain, Brunei, then outlying entities such as Madagascar, Mali, Maldives, and Vanuatu." Smith listed off the countries.

"Ah … he's right." Ethan—she believed Archangel had called him—said and then continued, "He forgot Bhutan, but he's absolutely correct."

"Where do we start?" Dom Ops asked.

"Alpha, is Tori able to work?" Archangel inquired.

"Not yet. Hopefully, soon."

"All right. We do this the old-fashioned way. I'll contact the Secretary of State and ask for downward-directed cooperation. Dom Ops, we'll need to pull in people who have been medically cleared to start working on the information we'll get in."

"I have a pool of people. It's been over four

months since the Siege, and they want to work. I'll put Kannon Starling in charge of it. Where do you want them to work?"

"Rent out a conference center. Make sure we have acceptable classified storage available. We'll sift for any information we can find."

"I'd go to Russia. From there, I could plan where to lay low," the Rose interjected.

"Not a good time to have people inside Russia."

"Not even people who could blend in?" Anubis asked.

Archangel made a sound of interest. "Explain that."

"Sunset Operative Thirteen speaks fluent Russian."

She nodded. She did.

"So do I," Smith said in perfect Russian. She blinked and lifted onto her elbows, dislodging the phone from where she'd set it. He shrugged.

"Well, there you go. They play like Russian citizens and be available if we need her to do her job."

"Do you have contacts in Russia and a reason to be there?"

She pushed her hair back. *Fuck*. "I do, and I can get an invitation without a problem." That was *not* what she wanted for Smith or herself.

"Get there. Fury, you work Smith's documentation, and Anubis, give Operative Thirteen whatever she needs."

"Done."

"On it," Anubis replied after Fury.

"How long will it take you to set up the invite?" Archangel spoke to her again.

"Could take up to a week. I can't press too hard. This crowd is spooky."

"We'll work the intel until you get an invite. We don't have a week. Archangel, out."

"Anubis, get me the requirements, and I'll work the logistics. The Rose is clear."

"Alpha out."

"Dom Ops is clear."

"Val, would going in alone be better? I can have Harbinger babysit Smith until his clearance is updated," Anubis asked.

She turned and looked at Smith. "No, he'll be an asset."

"All right. Annex is clear."

"CCS—"

"CCS, could you do me a favor? Can I talk to Bengal?" Val hurried to stop the young man from clearing the line.

"I'm here."

"I have it on exceptional authority that an anonymous man called the feds about a certain warehouse owned by Mrs. Henshaw's children. Seems they were into illegal activities. I'm really curious as to how that went down."

Bengal chuckled. "Smith. I should have guessed. When?"

"About one in the morning, New York time yesterday." Val glanced over at Smith, and he nodded.

"I'll look into it. You two stay safe. Don't play games you don't need to be involved with." Bengal warned.

She sighed. "You've played with the OPG?"

"Too many times."

"Once is too many." Val hated dealing with the Bratva. The Russian Mob was ruthless and would kill both of them if they suspected for a second that either was working for Guardian.

"We do whatever it takes." Bengal sighed.

"For as long as it takes. Good night." Val clicked off the call and flopped back onto Smith.

"The Bratva?"

"Yes. We have a lot to talk about. Let's do that over our dinner, which is no doubt cold by now."

Even though the food was room temperature, it was delicious. Smith took care to use the table manners he was taught eons ago. Val always made him want to be better. Which was next to impossible, but he tried.

"Where did you learn Russian?" Val asked from her side of the table.

"My mother." He took a sip of his water and leaned back. "She's Russian."

Val cocked her head. "Is she a first-generation American?"

"Yes." He took another bite of his steak.

Val scrunched her nose at him. "Are you going to make me pull the information from you?" She took a sip of her wine as she watched him. "I can, you know." She placed her hand on his. "Don't make me."

A small chuckle escaped him. She would. The woman was tenacious. "She met my father when he was doing some work in the oil fields of Russia. There was an educational exchange in the late seventies. Russia needed outside help to upgrade its crude oil infrastructure. My father met her the first time he was there. He went back three different times, and they fell in love. They devised a plan for her to leave Russia, and they were married in Switzerland before they moved back to the States. It took over a year to clear the diplomatic red tape for her to gain a visa." He took another sip of water.

Val pushed her sautéed vegetables around her plate. "What was her maiden name?"

"Solntesevskaya. Nadia Solntesevskaya." He watched Val's face fall, and her eyes widened.

"Are you serious?"

"I am. She's the daughter of Mikhail Solntesevskaya." His mother was Bratva royalty, or she was until she married his father. A fact he found out as an adult while reading at a library instead of shivering on the streets. The name Solntesevskaya was infamous.

He'd never met his mother's family, but he'd found her birth certificate in the closet while looking for Christmas gifts one year. He'd asked her who Nadia Solntesevskaya was. He'd never forget her reaction or the beating he'd gotten from his father. Soon after, he was sent to boarding school.

"Holy fuck. How did Guardian not know this?" Val stood up and started pacing. "What am I supposed to do with this?" she mumbled and turned, walking back and running her hand through her long white hair.

"Guardian may find out when they run this upgraded clearance. There wasn't much need for more than a typical background check when I was watching over Mrs. Henshaw. My mother's name was misspelled on the marriage certificate and the visa. She kept the spelling and became Nora Solsevski." He sighed and looked at the food in front of him, which had lost all its allure.

Val paced and turned. He watched her start to shake her head, and then she stopped, looking at him. "You can't go to Russia with me."

"Why?"

"Why? Did you seriously just ask me that?" Her arms flew up in the air, and she groaned. "Smith, you are *family*. What if someone found out?"

He narrowed his eyes at her, confused by her consternation. He was a golden ticket for her. He could open doors she'd never be able to access. He might even be able to find out information on Komal. "Wouldn't that be better for Guardian's cause?"

"What?" She looked at him as if he'd grown three heads.

"I can provide you access to the inside of the Bratva. Information for your agency."

"*Our* agency." She flopped down on the couch, and her silk robe fell open, revealing her long, lovely legs.

He let his glance linger for a moment before speaking, "Once they know, it'll again be *your* agency." He shrugged. "I'll return to my apartment if that's what you want." He'd offered his services, but he wouldn't push the issue. Perhaps it was best if he left and let her do what she needed. The man Guardian called Harbinger could fly him back.

"Not true. Guardian doesn't abandon its people." She leaned forward and dropped her head into her hands. Her fall of hair draped past her knees, and Val flipped it back. "We need to talk to Anubis."

"Why?"

"Because I can't hide this information. Management needs to know." She flopped back onto the couch.

Smith stood up and made his way to where she sat, crouching in front of her. "Then don't hide it. I'm a tool, like any other man you've used to complete your work. This one, Komal, is an animal who must be put down. If using my mother's family name will assist you in doing so, then do it. If I'm a hindrance, send me back to my existence." The road he was to travel seemed to be hers to decide.

She leaned forward and pushed his hair back from his forehead. "And if taking you into Russia places you in danger?"

He shrugged. "The greater good is more important."

She shook her head and whispered, "Is it?"

He took her hand and kissed her palm. "It is. It always will be. If my life, or death, can benefit humanity, it will be a small repayment for the evil I've done at the behest of others."

"I'll call them. In the morning." She leaned forward and kissed him. "Tonight is ours."

8

Jewell flopped into her chair and grabbed her juice just as the phone rang. She tapped the keyboard and answered the Annex's call. "CCS, what's up?" She never took off her headset while working, so she was ready to go at a moment's notice.

"I have an issue I need to run up the flagpole." Anubis' voice put her nerves on edge.

"What can I do?" She grabbed her juice and took a chug.

"We'll need all the information you have on the Solntesevskaya Brotherhood."

Jewell blinked and put the juice down. "The Bratva? Why? What's going on?"

"Sunset Operative Thirteen discovered that

Smithson Young is the son of Nadia Solntesevskaya. I need to know where she fell in the pecking order before she left Russia. Has there been communication between his mother and Smithson?"

Jewell's fingers raced as she typed. "Got it. Did he volunteer the information?"

"Yes."

"Well, that's a good sign," she muttered. She liked Smithson. He was quiet and respectful and took good care of Mrs. Henshaw.

"Can we expedite his clearance?"

Jewell looked up at her screens. "I know someone who owes me a big favor. I can call in that chip. It'll take twenty-four hours, but we'll have everything on Smithson Young, his family, and their pet parrot."

"Call it in, please." Anubis cleared his throat. "We all like Smithson, but if he's a plant, we need to know."

"Got it. What else?"

"Route me in with everyone? I'm not leaving this until later to brief it up."

She didn't blame him, especially with Guardian's one-time war and continuing skirmishes with the Bratva. That war had started when

Vista, the Russian hacker, had attacked her systems, back when Zane was just her caretaker-slash-bodyguard. "Okay, hold on." She put Anubis on hold, typed the request to call in a favor from her friend in the NSA, then sent out an all-call. As the participants started answering, she checked to ensure the calls were secure and took a sip of orange juice before telling them the line was clear. Time to be a fly on the wall.

Archangel barked, "Repeat that?"

"His mother is Nadia Solntesevskaya," Anubis repeated for Jewell's brother. She glanced at the clock. He should have had his coffee by now. Jason being a grump was not good for anyone. She smiled at her husband, Zane, or Bengal, as everyone knew him at Guardian, as he walked into the living room-slash-CCS. She could hardly wait to move to the Annex and spread out. They didn't have a place for a Christmas tree. Not even a small one, and Christmas was only a handful of months away. They had precious little space in the apartment and no privacy with Ethan living with them. Zane began to read the voice-to-text transcription she was running on the meeting. His eyes narrowed, and he sat beside her. "Damn."

She nodded and hit the button, putting the

conversation on speaker instead of her headphones.

“We can use him,” Jacob and Joseph said at the same time. Those brothers of hers were on the same page most of the time.

Jason grunted something, neither confirming nor dismissing his brothers’ comments. “Do we know how involved he is with the Brotherhood?”

“I’m pulling favors from the NSA. I’ll know what color his dog’s food bowl is by this time tomorrow.” Jewell glanced at the message she’d sent and smiled at the “done” she’d gotten in return. Super hackers had each other’s back no matter what organization they worked for. Well, the legal organizations, that was.

“He speaks fluent Russian. I say we get the information from Jewell’s contact, and if he’s good to go, we baptize him with fire. Put him in country with Val. We aren’t hunting Bratva. We’re hunting Komal.” Fury, her brother Joseph, said.

“Then, when we have that bastard taken care of, we regroup, and if possible, we can use him to go after the Bratva.” That was Jacob talking.

“We’re not at war with the Bratva right now, and I’m not ready to defend the walls if they do come after us,” Jewell reminded them. She didn’t need any more stress in her life. Working with limited capabilities and only herself and Ethan manning the fort was exhausting. There was never a down moment when she was in front of the keyboard. Her life consisted of work and sleep.

"Agreed. We don't want to start a war, but that doesn't mean we can't take proactive steps to prevent one in the future," her brother Jacob said.

"What do you mean, Alpha?" Anubis asked.

"A long-lost son of the Bratva returns. An introduction, an open door, a way in. We need to normalize the meeting. Have it casual, a comment overheard by someone with known connections and allegiance. They seek him out. We don't seek them out. In the meantime, we make subtle inquiries in the country about the mess in the Hague. Two birds, one stone."

"That sounds like a plan, but only if Jewell's contact clears Young. If he is, use that data to push his security clearance and bring him into the fold." Archangel gave the command.

"As a Sunset Operative?" Anubis asked.

There was a pause as everyone waited for Jason to make the call. Since the Siege, they'd been flying by the seat of their pants on a lot of issues.

That one was a sticky sucker. Jewell glanced at her husband and lifted her eyebrows. He shrugged.

"As Thirteen's bravo, her partner. They're now a team."

"Copy that," Anubis replied.

Jewell let out a breath. Her brother was a freaking genius. She wouldn't have thought of that.

Jason sighed. "Anything else?"

"Wasn't that enough?" Jewell quipped.

"It was," Jason agreed. "I'm late for my PT."

"Ah, that's why you're grumpy." Jewell slapped her hand over her mouth and stared wide-eyed at the computer screen.

All her brothers laughed. "Go do your exercises, grumpy pants. The Rose is clear."

"Alpha out."

"Dom Ops out."

"Annex Out."

"Love you, Jace," Jewell said to her brother when they were the last ones on the line.

"Love you, too, Button. Archangel out." Jason hung up.

"Well, that's a hell of a way to wake up," Zane said and leaned over to kiss her. "Breakfast?"

"I've got my juice."

"That's not breakfast." He stood up and walked

the short distance to the kitchen. “What’s burning a hole in our pocket today?”

Jewell glanced at the computerized to-do list and rolled her shoulders. “Five thousand and ten items.” She groaned inwardly. That was the scaled-down version of things that needed to be handled.

“And where do we start?” Zane asked as he took a frying pan from the cabinet.

“With the first one.” She nodded. She was overwhelmed a lot lately. Thank God for Zane and Ethan’s help. Zane took each new request from the field and prioritized them, so she didn’t have to worry about what came next. What she wouldn’t give for her entire section to be back. She batted away that sorrow and clicked on the top folder. Time to make as much of a dent as she could.

9

Smith winced and closed his eyes. Riding in a car in London was not a pleasant experience. In his personal opinion, the knee-jerk reaction to being on the wrong side of the road was akin to nails on a chalkboard. He placed the sunglasses Val had purchased and packed for him on even though it wasn't sunny. They gave him plausible deniability. He closed his eyes when they entered a traffic circle.

Val must have looked over at him because she laughed. "You'll get used to it. I remember my first time driving in London. I almost hyperventilated, but thankfully, I learned in the villages and progressed to more and more congested roadways.

I still make the occasional foible, but nothing that has killed anyone yet."

"Thank God," he mumbled, and Val's laughter again filled the car. "We're almost out of the worst traffic."

He opened one eye as she turned ... into the wrong lane ... and snapped it shut. His head dropped back to the headrest. They hadn't slept much last night, which was two nights of inadequate sleep for him. He smiled. He'd lose sleep any time if it involved her in his bed.

"What are you smiling about?"

He spoke without opening his eyes. "Remembering last night and the fact that I'm tired, but I can't say I'm sorry about my current situation."

"I'm not sorry about it either." She purred the response. "See, open road. You can look now."

Smith lifted his head and looked around. "This cottage is a what? A safe house?"

"Exactly. I have them in several major cities. Rent is paid through a shell company not associated with me. I stock them with arms, ammunition, clothes, food, and, most importantly, new identification. Guardian wipes me from transportation facial recs as a matter of routine. When I travel, I let management know, and they input the information to our computer specialists. Since we're a hidden resource, we're a priority. Guardian is very careful to wipe out any information about us that they don't want to be made public."

"Which is why there was such emphasis on keeping you out of anyone's focus when we landed." Smith nodded before he asked, "Are you supposed to be telling me this?" He'd made himself scarce during her call that morning and the subsequent return conversation. It was the longest shower he'd taken in years, but the five showerheads helped him forget his status was still in question with Guardian.

Val glanced over at him. Once again, she'd transformed into a brunette with brown eyes and the lifts in her shoes that made her almost six feet tall. "I thought you'd never ask about what they said on the call."

He drew back a bit. "I didn't. I asked if you were authorized to tell me what you have."

"Close enough." Val waved a hand in the air. "Okay, so this is the gist. When your clearance or investigation comes through tomorrow morning, you get to be my partner for this operation." She nodded to herself and put on the blinker marking her intent to exit the road.

Smith considered the words for a moment. "I thought I was working with you already. What aren't you telling me?"

She glanced over at him and winked. "That's top secret. I'll tell you when your clearance comes through."

He nodded. Rational, if not a little unsettling. Val turned again and drove down a road leading them into the countryside. The clouds parted, and the sun streamed through the windshield. It was a beautiful area, and he'd been raised in a rural town like it. Vast land between houses used to be the norm. The last time he'd driven by his childhood house, the once-vacant areas were filled with new mini-mansions. His father and mother had painted and renovated since he left. However, the iron gate that blocked the driveway was still adorned with the "Y," indicating they still owned the property.

"How often have you practiced your Russian?" Val asked him in the language.

He replied in kind. "Often. Whenever I visit Brighton Beach, which everyone calls Little Odessa, I speak only Russian. There are several restaurants in New York, Russian neighborhoods, and enforcers who do the same thing as me, and I converse with them." He extended his answer because he knew she wanted to see how proficient he was with the language. "What about you?" he asked, still speaking in Russian.

"I learned it when I joined Guardian. French, Italian, and Russian. Those are the countries where I'm most utilized." She shrugged. "I'm trying to learn Arabic. It's a work in progress." Her pronunciation was fluid, and her accent was neutral.

Smith continued in Russian. "Do you say you're American?"

She glanced at him. "Depends on the mission. Americans aren't hated in Russia. American politics are. Americans have money and sometimes contacts that are hard for certain people inside Russia to make. Through Guardian, I've supplied valuable information. My acquaintances are on the Bratva fringe, and I've never been questioned or accosted. Well, except for once."

"What happened?" He'd gladly twist the head off anyone with the balls to accost Val.

"A young Brigadier within the Bratva wanted access to the political influence he thought I had. I refused his command and told the young man to grow up before he played with the big boys."

"How did that go over?" He could only imagine the young man's wounded pride.

"There was a heated discussion." She shrugged. "He didn't worry me. He was just a young bull trying to push me around. I can handle myself."

Smith chuckled, and her head whipped in his direction. "Do you doubt my capabilities?"

He glanced over at her. "No. I'm sure you handle weapons very well."

She snorted. "I'm better with my hands."

"That you are." As he recalled vividly from last night.

She rolled her eyes. "Thank you, but no, not that. I could take you down. Quickly, I might add." She slowed and signaled to turn down a gravel road.

That time, he laughed. "I saw the hijacker on the aircraft. The damage you inflicted was apparent."

"Yet, I still hear the doubt in your voice." Val glanced at him before pointing through the windshield. "That's mine. It's an old Mill cottage. Over that hill is the Manor House. The owners are elderly and just wanted a steady rental income. I'm rarely here, so they aren't inconvenienced.

They can pay their bills, and I keep the place nice."

Smith took in the view of the small house. It was two stories, built of stone with a roof that sagged just a bit between the two windows of the second floor. A red frame and the same color front door between two larger windows looked inviting. The grounds were meticulously maintained.

"I have a contract with the manor owner's landscaping company." Val seemed to know what he was thinking, which would have been irritating with anyone else. He prided himself on his lack of expression. She put the vehicle in Park, and Smith gratefully pulled himself out of the front seat. He rolled his shoulders and stretched to the cloud-covered sky, his back popping several times. "Would you get the basket from the boot, please?" Val asked as she headed to the cottage.

He obliged, pulling what looked like an oversized picnic basket out of the back of the car. He ducked down to enter the little house and was pleasantly surprised at the inside. A small sofa and a large, overstuffed chair were positioned in front of the recessed wood-burning stove. The ceilings were higher than he'd expected and were adorned with exposed beams. Underfoot, he stood on quarry tiling. There was a rug in front of the couch and chair.

All in all, it was a nice place. The kitchen was small and functional. He heard footsteps upstairs.

"I'll be right down," Val called out.

Smith put the basket on the kitchen counter and exited the cottage, taking in the view from the front door. A small wooden bridge spanned a brook where he assumed the old mill must have been located. The trees were full of leaves and turning colors. There was a crisp feel in the air and no noise except for the sound of birds in the trees, the light babble of water in the brook, and the ripple of a breeze through the leaves. A cornerstone placed at the base of the small cottage marked the year 1560. He gazed at the huge trees and wondered if any had seen the place being built.

"Beautiful, isn't it?" Val said from behind him.

"It is. Peaceful." He nodded.

"Okay, so we have lunch. Inside or al fresco?"

"Do you think the rain will hold off?" He nodded at the clouds.

"Who knows? I'm willing to gamble if you are." She leaned against him. "We'll stay close."

"All right, I'll grab the basket."

"I'll get a blanket." They moved around and out of the cottage together. God, he wanted to put his arm around her as they strolled, but he had no idea if she'd welcome that type of closeness. Besides, Guardian could pull the plug on him in the morning. God only knew what they'd find in their investigation. His family was almost a mystery to him, and that was how he liked it. His father and mother had turned him out and expected him to make his own way. He'd survived.

Val spread the blanket out, and they sat on it as she pulled out container after container of food. "Dinner wasn't great, and we skipped breakfast. I'm starving." She took out a bottle of wine, a bottle of water, and a small flask. "Your scotch, sir." Val shook the silver container. "We're off the clock and free of any interruptions here. A safe place to cut loose and relax."

"Until the morning," he acknowledged. "Did you reach your Russian contacts?"

"That's on hold until your expedited investigation gets back to management." Val popped an olive into her mouth and chewed it. "Any reason why you wouldn't pass muster?"

Smith picked up a sandwich made on a

baguette and took a bite. After he swallowed, he shook his head. "I don't know."

Val picked up her half of the sandwich and stalled with it halfway to her mouth. "What exactly does that mean?"

Smith took another bite. He didn't want to get into his childhood, but that ship had launched when he'd agreed to go on the trip with her, hadn't it? "After I found the information about my mother when I was six, I was sent to Preston Heights Military Academy, where I lived except for one month at Christmas until I graduated at eighteen."

She put her sandwich down on a piece of wax paper. "No other holidays or summers at home?"

"No." He lifted his eyes and saw the pity in hers. "Don't do that. Don't feel sorry for me. It is what it is."

She snorted. "Your parents are troglodytes."

Smith blinked and then laughed. "They don't live in a cave."

"No, but they acted like it. How could you send a child away like that? I can't have kids, but let me tell you, if I ever did, they'd be showered in love." She picked up her sandwich and took a huge bite, mumbling something as she chewed.

"I knew nothing different."

"Have you talked to anyone in your family since you left?"

"No. I haven't spoken to my family since my father told me to make my own way at the age of eighteen and asked me to leave."

She stopped chewing and swallowed hard. "That still pisses me off."

He grabbed a handful of chips and popped one in his mouth. "It is what it is."

She popped up to her knees and almost shouted, "What? No." Val sputtered, "*Oh my God*. I'm going to pay a visit to your parents." She shook her head and dropped back onto her butt. "I don't hate many people, but I think I'm leaning in that direction with your folks. They wouldn't like me when I'm mad." Val mumbled a few non-ladylike adjectives as she munched on several chips.

He shrugged. "Hate consumes too much energy." He only hated one person, and that bastard was dead. He'd helped incinerate Simmons' body. He was a nightmare that would never return.

"Stop being so *zen* about it. You should go back and show them you survived and that you're working for Guardian now." Val grabbed the wine opener from the basket.

Smith took the sharp object from the fiery

woman and opened her wine. "What reason would that serve? He'd think he was right in turning me out."

She stopped chewing and looked up at him. "Well, crud ... There is that."

After handing her a glass of the wine, he took another bite out of his sandwich. "Why can't you have children?"

Val stared at her wine for a moment. "I was married before I worked for Guardian. My husband didn't want kids. A really long, drawn-out story, but I agreed with him and had my tubes tied. Let me tell you, *that* was a fight. Doctors didn't want to do that procedure on a young woman, but we persisted and found someone who would perform the operation. My husband was murdered about a year later. That's when my world shattered into a million pieces."

"You must have loved him very much." Smith saw the grief in her expression, and *that* type of emotion was only reserved for those who were truly loved.

She looked straight at him. "I did. He's been gone for twelve years now. He'll always hold a special place in my heart." She drew a deep breath. "But life goes on."

"It does. What did he do when you lived in Minnesota?" Smith took another bite of his sandwich.

"Ha! Wrong. That's where I went to school. I moved to New York after I graduated, much to my parents' displeasure. I worked in a gym and started training. That's when I met him. He was a professional MMA fighter—a heavyweight. I also fought professionally. We trained together." She took a drink of her wine.

"Ah." Smith nodded. "Hence the statement, you could take me down easily."

"I said quickly, not easily, I believe." Val wagged a finger at him.

Smith took another bite of his sandwich, covering his smile. She'd said quickly. He changed the subject. "The house you live in was built in 1560."

She nodded. "A long time ago. I can't imagine what life then was like."

"It was a time of treachery and war. Queen Elizabeth the First successfully fought multiple attempts to usurp her. Protestants and Catholics were divided by events of the time, both in the church and politics. Life was not easy."

Val wrapped her arms around her knees and

stared into the small meadow. "It never is, it seems."

"Easy times make weak men." He believed that old saying. Strength came from adversity and hardships.

She nodded. "The people I've ..." she glanced up at him, then continued, "... dealt with for Guardian have money and power. The preponderance have no spine. With no fortitude, they send minions to do their bidding. Evil men are never as strong as those who struggle against them."

Smith laid back on the blanket and watched the gray clouds churn above him. "I was one of those minions."

She startled. "I didn't mean—"

He put a hand on her arm. "I know, but I agree with you. Evil men have an internal need, or perhaps a sickness, that drives them to do whatever it takes to pass as strong. To make people fear them."

Val held out her hand. "Is it raining?"

A sprinkle pelted him on the cheek. He sat up. "It is." Looking over the meadow, he pointed. "We're about to be very wet." Sheets of rain were visible across the brook.

"Crud," Val exclaimed. They chucked everything into the basket and took off at a run to the house. About halfway, the rain caught them, and they were soaking wet by the time they made it to the cottage.

Val started stripping at the front door. "Take your clothes off. We'll need to dry them in front of the fire." She hopped on one foot as she pulled her wet slacks off. Smithson reached behind him and pulled off his shirt.

Val was in front of him, naked. She reached for his belt and unfastened it and his slacks. The shirt hit the tile with a wet splat. He ran his hand through her hair, pulling off the wet wig and shaking her hair loose, letting it fall to her shoulders. He toed off his shoes and stepped out of his slacks when they hit the floor. "Where's the bedroom?"

"Upstairs." Val lifted to her toes and kissed his chin. He covered her lips with his and leaned down, lifting her off her feet. He broke the kiss to maneuver through the unfamiliar house. The stairs led to a loft bedroom with a king-sized bed, which he laid her down on. Smith had never had an addiction. He didn't understand those who did until then. The physical high he flew on when he was with her was ambrosia … something he'd fight for. Yes, he could see how addiction worked.

Their tongues danced, and she pushed on him. He lifted immediately.

"On your back." She pushed him with one finger, and he moved, rolling off her. She straddled him and resumed the kiss. He caressed her soft skin, drawing a finger up her ribcage. Her skin shivered under his touch and his tightened under hers. Smithson didn't know how long they touched and kissed. It could have been minutes or hours before she circled his cock and slowly lowered herself onto him. He grabbed her shoulders, and his legs shook with the effort it took not to thrust. His cock was a diamond-hard, greedy son of a bitch, but he kept still as she lifted and lowered. She took his hands and placed them on her breasts. He opened his eyes that had somehow closed and watched as her body literally danced on him. She was sensuous, nimble, and fluid, and the feel of her moving while he forced his body to remain still was erotic as hell.

His breath was coming in ragged pulls by the time she lost her rhythm. She opened her eyes and looked at him. A faint sound from her was all he needed. He rolled them and lifted her leg, pushing into her using a rapid, sharp movement. She grabbed his shoulders, arched her back, and yelled, "Yes!"

At that moment in time, he was the king of the world. Nothing or no one could have told him differently. He pushed himself as he drove into her. He couldn't hold back, and he sure as hell didn't want to. She shattered just as he did. The combined sensation of her body tightening around him as he shot was beyond anything he'd ever experienced. He rested his head against her pillow as he caught his breath, his weight held up on his elbow. When he could think again, he let go of her leg. It flopped to the bed, and she chuckled. "I can't feel them yet."

He lifted his head and met her gaze. "Did I hurt you?"

She gave a winded laugh, "Not a chance."

He leaned to his side and pulled her with him as he went. She yawned. "We should hang the clothes up and start a fire." Val tucked under his chin and pulled the covers over them.

"In a minute." He wrapped her in his arms, perfectly content and happy. It was a sensation that didn't often happen in his life. For once, he just wanted to close his eyes and enjoy the feeling.

10

Jewell King glanced over at the message board she used to communicate with other people in her profession. It wasn't exactly a legal system. Her standalone dark net computer was shielded and impossible for anyone to access. Still, all super hackers used the dark web, and she kept up with her contemporaries. A new message blinked in solidarity.

> QOTK TIRL ASAP CON

SHE LEANED FORWARD and read it again. "Ruh-roh, Scooby."

"Problems?" her husband said from his tiny desk tucked in the corner of what was once their living room. Man, they needed to move to the Annex. The work was almost done there. She and Zane would live in the underground facility, and Ethan would have his own apartment. She couldn't wait for the place to be done. She was starting to feel claustrophobic. Plus, she hated being in Washington. *Hated it.* The farther she was from the old Guardian building, the better. The memories were too fresh, too vivid, and all too deadly.

"What's wrong?" Zane was beside her, causing her to jump. "Hey, easy. I thought something was wrong."

"No, I was lost in my thoughts. That's what caught my attention." She pointed to the message board.

Zane bent down and read the message. He stood and rubbed his neck. "I understood ASAP. I have no idea what the rest of that means."

Jewell hadn't even thought to translate. Zane was such a quick study, but yeah, they did have their own language. She lumped herself in with the super hackers of the world. "Oh, QOTK is me. Queen of the keyboard. TIRL is talk in real life. ASAP you got. Con is his handle. He wants to talk."

She shoved her nail in her mouth and started to bite it.

Zane rubbed her shoulders. “Why is that bad?”

“He’s the person I know who works in the NSA. I asked him to do a rush investigation on Smithson Young, but we’ve never spoken. I’ve known him for ten or fifteen years but never talked to him. It’s kind of … weird.” She didn’t know if talking was a good idea.

Zane kissed the top of her head. “So call him. I’ll be here.”

“Yeah, not that easy. I don’t have his number. Hold on.”

She pulled the sliding keyboard out of the tray of the shielded computer and typed.

> Now.

She sat back and looked at the phone. Three seconds later, it rang. “That’s freaky,” Zane mumbled.

She picked up the receiver. “That was quick.”

“I was waiting.” The deep timbre of the hacker on the other side of the connection wasn’t how she'd imagined he'd sound. Somehow, in her mind, she pegged him as an acne-marked teenager with a nasally, whiny voice, even after fifteen years.

She shook off the surprise. "You've got me. What's up?"

"First, I'm glad that fucker didn't kill you when the building went up in smoke."

She swallowed and looked at her husband. "It was a close call. I lost most of my team."

"I heard. Keep me in mind when you start rebuilding. I'm losing my mind in the tedium over here. Which leads me to the reason for the call. Thank you for giving me something interesting to amuse myself. Since POTUS directed us to support Guardian, I put away all the other mind-dulling must-dos and focused on your Smithson Young."

"Wait. You can't drop a bomb like that. You'd come to work for us?" Jewell looked at her husband and smiled wide.

"Yeah, of course. Brando and Ring would, too. We were discussing that the other night over drinks."

"What? Do you guys know each other? Why haven't you invited me for drinks?" She may or may not have shrieked that.

The smooth laugh that came over the connection didn't assuage her shock. "Well, for one, we don't know who you are. Brando is my brother, and Ring is our cousin. So we get together occasionally. D.C. is an exceedingly small place."

"If you're serious, when Guardian is ready, I'll float a message to you. But it could be up to a year, and the concept will be different than how we manage things now."

"Makes sense. No promises, but I'll take a serious look at moving."

"The money's good," Jewell added.

"We both know we don't do this for the money. It's the thrill."

"Amen," she agreed. "Now, what about Smithson?"

"Okay, I'm sending this through secure channels, which means management is going to delay it getting to you, but no one said I couldn't brief you on what I found."

She chuckled. "Did you ask?"

"Why would I?" He laughed. "Better to ask for forgiveness than beg for permission. Besides, I don't beg. So there's that."

"All right, I'm ready. Spill."

Zane wheeled his chair over beside her and grabbed a tablet and paper. He was so funny. Cute, even. She grabbed his pen and shoved it over her ear, lodging it in the locks of her messy bun as she called up a document and activated the dictation program.

"Smithson Dimitri Young, only son to James Smithson Young and Nora Solsevski Young. And that's the first wrinkle in this investigation. Nora is actually Nadia Solntesevskaya, as in the Bratva's missing darling. She was engaged to be married to one of the oligarchs at the time. This guy was like sixty-five and butt ugly but also very powerful in the politburo and high-ish in the Bratva. He was not as high as the Solntesevskayas, but he had ambition when he was young and obtained political connections.

"Needless to say, he wasn't a happy camper when Nadia disappeared, and a divide in the Bratva caused by her running off still exists today. The Solntesevskayas and the Molotovs, yes, like the cocktail, are at odds. The Solntesevskayas are larger and have more assets. Of the three million known members of the brotherhood, the Solntesevskayas control a branch with over seven hundred fifty thousand members. None of the other branches of the Bratva come close. They are the largest criminal syndicate in the world."

"Wait, how did she meet Smithson's old man?" Jewell leaned forward, completely enthralled with the story.

"Glad you asked. He traveled to Russia in the seventies, no less, on an educational exchange. They met then. Young has money. By all accounts, he's a smart guy and had a sweet gig with one of the major oil companies. Mid to high six-figure income until about fifteen years ago. Then new money started pouring in based on technology he's invented and copyrighted. Some gadget that revolutionized refineries in the oil industry. The thing is, he was sued by another person who claimed he was the actual inventor of the device. The man went missing, and the case never went to court."

"Interesting," Jewell commented. "What about Smithson?"

"Man, this guy's life has sucked in a major way. And I say that having lived an ultra-sucky life. The exclusive and extremely expensive boarding school your Smithson attended has digital records. Which was a score in the good column for them, but they had zero meaningful safeguards. My dog could have hacked their system. I managed to get all of the younger Smithson's records. It wasn't a happy read. His sperm donor paid two times the going rate of tuition to keep him there eleven months out of the year. His progress reports indicate he's very intelligent but a loner. He got straight A's in school, volunteered for every extra credit assignment, and blew the SATs out of the fucking water. The school kept their correspondence with the parents. The academy refused to keep him over the Christmas and New Year holidays, stating their staff needed a break. He couldn't apply for college without his parents' information because they made too much money, which disqualified him from any grants. The scholarships he was offered were withdrawn. I cracked into those colleges. The parents made hefty donations, and the scholarships were pulled. Those fuckers made sure nobody wanted the kid."

"Damn." Jewell shook her head. She couldn't imagine growing up alone without the love that her mom had made sure was available.

"Yeah. About three weeks after he graduated, I started finding police reports from New York City with his name. The charges run the gambit from vagrancy, petty theft, and brawling. He's heir to a multi-million-dollar fortune. What in the hell was he doing on the streets of New York? I had to ask myself, did he run away from those shit parents?

There are gaps of years before there are mentions of him as a suspect in numerous crimes, but nothing was pinned on him. We're talking murder charges here. Six that I've uncovered. Then nothing until about ten years ago. It looks like your Smithson straightened out some and worked for a minor politician named Simmons in New York, according to payroll records. I'm finding some pretty shady dealings attached to this guy Simmons, so maybe your guy didn't actually straighten up but became a higher-class form of killer. From there, tracking him has been exceptionally spotty. He's been off the grid. I can't tell you who's paying him if he's getting a check. If he has a cell phone it is pay-as-you-go. No contracts in his name. There are no credit cards, no debt, and no bank accounts that I can find. I assume his housing is paid in cash, as I don't have any rental agreements. He's pretty damn good at ghosting, although facial rec picked him up on a flight to London. Guess which flight?"

"The New York to London flight that hijackers attempted to take over," Jewell answered.

"Damn it. You knew." There was a sigh. "How?"

"I have to keep some of my secrets, but the rest of the information is exactly what we need." Jewell nodded to herself. "All right. So, nothing notorious or anything that would stop him from being cleared?"

"Haven't you been listening to me? I wouldn't clear him, and I can one hundred percent guarantee the Office of Personnel Management won't give this guy a clearance. He has a criminal background and is a suspect in at least six open felony murder cases. Granted, they're all cold cases, but still."

"Suspected, right? Not convicted."

"Yep. Guilty until proven innocent, especially with our judicial system." Con chuckled.

"That's not the way it's supposed to go." Jewell rolled her eyes even though the guy couldn't see it. "Anything else?"

"Well, not with him, but remember that missing tech guy?"

"Yeah, the one suing his dad."

"The Youngs started making overseas calls a month before that guy disappeared. Guess where they called."

"Russia."

"Bingo. All calls trace to Pappa Solntesevskaya. Putting two and two together and seeing the total of a missing person at the end, it looks like the princess called Daddy for a little old-fashioned Bratva intervention. The communications have become more frequent as time has passed, and the Youngs have traveled back to Mother Russia numerous times. As a matter of fact, they're currently in Russia."

Jewell frowned. That was really hard to pin as a coincidence. Both Smithson and his parents were overseas at the same time. Why *was* Smithson going overseas? She needed more information because the dots didn't connect. Yet. "Do you know where the Youngs are currently?"

"Based on their past spending, it could be anywhere from Krasnoyarsk to Moscow to St. Petersburg. They travel extensively inside the country. I haven't hacked into Russia in a long time, but it's not hard. I think whatever rift Nadia caused by leaving has been repaired, at least on her side of the divide."

"Cool. Thanks. I have an off-topic question. Any idea where Komal is heading?"

There was a pause before Con cleared his throat. "Yes, that is correct."

"Russia? Someone just came into your office, didn't they?"

"Yes, that's right. You are following the right protocols. Is there anything else you need?"

"Nope. Thanks a billion." She stopped the transcription, and the connection ended without Con saying another word. "So Smithson doesn't have a stellar record." She bit her lip.

"You know his past isn't the issue. It's the present, his future, and his abilities they're going to examine. He has a few bumps in the road, but we've worked with more damaged people." Zane sighed. "Usually, the recruiter puts them through a scrub. We don't have that luxury."

She nodded and glanced at her husband. He was her center, her true north. "Do I go forward with the verbal brief or wait for the approved version from the NSA?"

"We go forward. Komal is the most wanted man in the world, and minutes matter. His attacks killed scores of innocents in the Netherlands. He's abducted almost half a million children and subjected them to the horrors of war and prostitution. I know your brother will want this information. He needs to get assets moving, so he'd want it sooner rather than later." Zane made her life so easy, and he made sense of the world on the other side of her computer screens.

Jewell nodded and pulled up the transcribed document. "I'll clean this up and blast it out to everyone involved. That'll save me from telling everyone the same thing repeatedly."

"Smart. I'm going to wake up Ethan. He has a test he needs to log in and take."

Jewell made a grunt of disapproval. "That class is so below his skillset."

"Now, and thanks to you." Zane chuckled. "Are you set here?"

"I'm good." She moved forward and bumped her knee. She rubbed it and griped, "Ouch. Man, I'm hoping the Annex is ready sooner rather than later."

"We should be there in less than a month. I promise bigger and better things are coming your way. Can you hang on that long? Maybe Santa will bring you something special, too." Zane bent down and kissed her.

"Santa doesn't need to get me anything. With you by my side, I can do anything." She truly believed that.

He smiled at her and dropped for another kiss. "Be right back."

She watched him walk away, then turned back to

her document. With Smithson's criminal history, he wouldn't get a standard clearance from the Office of Personnel Management. But then again, for what he was doing and who he was with, he didn't need a standard clearance. His criminal history would probably be attributed to the gain column rather than a loss tally. But ultimately, that wasn't her decision. Archangel, Fury, and Lycos would have to make that call. Sunset Operatives were their territory.

~

VAL WOKE SUDDENLY alert and lifted her head, looking at the man with her. Smithson Young. He was such a sexy savage. She relaxed and lowered her head. He'd finally shown her how strong he was. She ached in all the best places. The tentativeness the man held her with needed to go. She wasn't fragile or breakable.

She rolled over and snuggled into his warm body. Rain pelted the windows, and she could see rivulets run along the glass. It was getting dark, so they'd been asleep for a couple of hours, at least. She knew the moment Smith woke. "We slept," she whispered.

"We did," he whispered back, pulling her against him a little tighter.

"I liked it when you lost a little bit of that iron-clad self-control you brandish about like a weapon."

Val felt him stiffen immediately. "I didn't hurt you, did I?"

She turned in his arms. "No. I enjoyed it. I'd tell you if I didn't." She rested on her arm, and he did the same. "You don't have to be careful around me. I'd tell you if I didn't like something we did." The tension seemed to release from his body at her reassurance. She watched his reaction, which, other than releasing tension from his body, was no reaction. That meant his defenses were up. He was a master at masking what he was thinking or feeling.

She lifted an eyebrow. "One day, I'll get you to trust me."

His jaw twitched, and he looked confused as he told her, "I've told you more about myself than I've ever told any other living soul. You're the only person I've opened up to."

She lifted her finger and traced his bottom lip. "But you still don't trust me."

He moved back a bit, and her finger dropped. "Do you trust me?"

She lifted to her elbow and looked down at him. She could tell him a lie, but he'd know it. "I trust you as much as I trust anyone."

He smiled at that. "Perhaps one day we'll trust each other."

She smiled. "Guarded people, aren't we?"

"We have the right to be," he agreed.

"We do. I need to rescue our clothes from molding to the tile floor." She sat up and stretched. "Bathroom is in there. I'll meet you in a couple of minutes if you start the shower."

"Deal." Smithson lifted out of bed and headed into the bathroom. She watched his muscled back, ass, and thick thighs the entire way. Drool-worthy.

Val popped downstairs, shut the front door, which they'd left open, and mopped up the water pooling from the blowing rain. The fire was set and ready to light. It took several minutes for her to get the clothes hung on kitchen chairs and placed in front of the fire, which was licking happily at the dry wood in the cast iron belly of the stove. She turned and headed toward the stairs, and that's when she heard the phone vibrate. "Aw, damn it." *They really knew how to ruin a lazy rainy day, didn't they?*

Val answered the call, authenticated, and was placed on standby immediately. She walked upstairs and opened the bathroom door. Smith wiped at the steamy glass of the shower enclosure and peered out at her. She pointed to the phone and crooked her finger at him.

He turned off the water and slicked back his hair, swiping most of the moisture from it. She handed him a towel and watched him dry off. Damn, if there weren't people on the line, she'd drop to her knees and make that mountain of a man tremble.

They moved into the bedroom, and Smith dropped onto the bed, leaning against the headboard. She knee-walked across the bed to where he was sitting and leaned back against him instead of the cold, carved, wooden headboard.

She put the phone on speaker, and they listened as everyone onboarded.

"CCS online, and the connection is secure." CCS ended the attendance portion of the call.

"Is Smithson there?" Archangel's voice growled across the connection.

"I am," he answered immediately.

"I'm going to cut to the chase. You're a suspect in six felonies. All murders. All in New York City. Did you commit them?"

Smith looked over at her. "I've committed four times that number."

Val kept eye contact with him as he spoke. It was obvious he wanted to see if his words impacted her. They didn't. She'd killed. He'd killed. It was a job for both of them. The past was not what they were focusing on. There was silence for a prolonged period of time. Val covered the mic with the pad of her finger. "They're discussing what you just said with us muted out. Lycos is the recruiter responsible for people who do what I do. He's going to weigh in on whether or not he thinks you're salvageable," She shrugged.

His eyes narrowed, but he nodded, and they continued to wait. "Smithson, we are discussing your loyalty to Guardian and the nation," Archangel said, breaking the muted silence.

Smithson blinked at the statement. "I do not cherish the thought of an initiation al la Bratva. However, if required, I would be willing to prove it through an initiation ritual. Guardian has been faithful to me. I will be faithful to it."

Val frowned. When she was recruited, either

you agreed to work for Guardian or didn't. If you didn't, you were turned over for your crimes and never heard from Guardian again. There was a bark of laughter, and then Fury said, "See, I told you. I like this guy."

"Thanks for the input." Archangel's words said one thing, and his tone said another. "Loyalty to us is essential."

"I would assume it is," Smithson acknowledged. "Is this initiation required by all of your employees?"

Val shook her head and mouthed "no" at the same time as Archangel said the word. He continued, "To help you understand our concern, we've received an initial debrief on your security investigation. When was the last time you contacted your parents?"

Smithson's muscles tightened under her. "The last time I saw either of them was when they kicked me out of their home. I had enough money to buy a bus ticket to New York. I had the hope of finding a job. I didn't, and life wasn't that easy for me."

"That was obvious due to your arrest record. To verify, you've had no recent contact with your parents or sisters?"

Smith drew a breath and replied, "Sir, my parents wanted nothing to do with me. I was abandoned at a boarding school. They tolerated my presence one month a year. During those times, there were no happy family outings or magical Christmas miracles. I have driven by my family home three times since I left. The last time was the day after Mrs. Henshaw died. That drive confirmed that Mrs. Henshaw was more of a mother figure in my life than my biological mother had ever been. Additionally, I. Don't. Lie. Check those felony cases. I did not spin any fabrications. I exercised my constitutional right under the fifth amendment and remained completely silent. My employers, who had far more to lose than I did, made the situations disappear."

Val could hear tapping in the background, and then there was silence. Archangel spoke again after about two minutes. "Pending a routine psychological evaluation and based on your complete honesty, I'm going to grant you a probationary Sunset clearance. Val, you and Smithson will proceed with all haste to Russia. All intelligence and police agencies in Europe are looking for Komal. According to our allies in other agencies, all the chatter is that he's already in Russia."

"Where do you want us?"

"Novosibirsk," Fury interjected.

"New Siberia?" Val translated the city's name into English.

"We have the other cities covered via sister organizations in other countries. However, there's a credible source, the air marshal that you took down, who stated it is rumored that Komal is going to China, where he'll wait until he can relocate."

"Why not stay in Russia?" the woman from CCS asked.

"Political tensions are extremely high, especially with the Russian border war. No one wants to be caught in Russia if things go sideways. Plus, Komal has purported ties to the Triad through his sex trafficking operation. Going to where friends have a stronghold makes sense," Archangel explained.

"Are you thinking he'll ride the Trans-Siberian railroad to Beijing? Novosibirsk is the halfway point of that journey." Val popped the question. That would be the only reason Guardian would send them to Novosibirsk. The railway was the only efficient way to get from the eastern part of Russia to Beijing in short order. Unless you flew,

Siberia's airports with refueling capabilities were few and far between.

Fury answered, "To us, it's the most logical assumption and one the other agencies are not actively pursuing. We've got comm devices and Russian passports heading your way, along with a complete threat package. The courier will be in London in less than nine hours. We have a strawman operation built. Do you need any hardware?"

"No. I can access everything we'll need." Val dropped her head back on his shoulder. "Standard reporting?"

"If you can without being compromised," Anubis instructed. Val acknowledged the command. Russia didn't trust its citizens and routinely monitored most conversations conducted over a cell phone. It also tried to control access to the internet, so the government's rhetoric was the only conversation heard by its population.

She sat up, holding the sheet in place, and asked, "What are the scheduled runs on the train route, and would he take a private passenger train rather than hoboing it on a supply train?"

"Komal is by all intelligence reports extremely narcissistic and considers himself a man of extreme worth. He wouldn't dream of riding in a supply car. Regarding which train, we're working that through eyes on the ground in Moscow," Archangel advised.

All right. She could work with that. "Anything else?" Val was ready to end the call and start planning what she could of the operation.

"Yes. Smithson, your parents are in Russia. Apparently, whatever rift was between your mother's family and your parents seems to have been mended."

Smith nodded and lifted a hand in the air. "This is why you were concerned about my loyalty to Guardian. The timing of my being in Europe and their travels."

"It seemed too coincidental to some of us. You conveniently being in Europe while your parents are in Russia raised eyebrows," Fury acknowledged.

"I understand. Guardian has my loyalty. I owe those people nothing."

Val patted his arm. "Besides that, Smithson didn't know he was coming to Europe until I took him to the airport, so there was no timing, plan, or intent on his part. I planned the trip and basically kidnapped him. He had no idea where we were going or why. He's just along for the ride."

There was a low rumble of laughter that she couldn't identify. "Good to know." She recognized Lycos' voice as he spoke for the first time.

"Val, report your concerns on the preliminary strawman operation after you review the package. We'll run the table," Anubis reminded her. Running the table played devil's advocate with the plan, making it stronger or trashing it altogether if it didn't hold water through the discussion.

"Affirmative. My contacts are in St. Petersburg and will be of no help. We'll be going in solo."

"Understood and anticipated. Be advised Komal is coded." Archangel delivered the sweetest permission with those words.

"I copy." She'd gladly end that bastard. Unfortunately, they had to find him before every other agency in the free world.

They cleared the call, and she crossed her arms over her sheet-covered breasts. "Why Novosibirsk? Why not sooner?"

"I would assume to give him time to settle, to think he's made it undetected." Smith postulated.

"We won't know if there are other operatives on

the train. It could get messy." Val pulled her hand through her hair.

"I've been messy before." Smith shrugged, and her body moved with his.

"So have I. Tell me, Mr. Young, do you have a preference when it comes to a weapon? I don't have a Colt like you carry at home."

He shook his head. "Any large caliber handgun will suffice."

"Then, come on, we have some flooring to move."

11

Smith slid out of the car before the valet could open his door and went to the trunk of the vehicle, grabbing the picnic basket they'd taken to the cottage. It was no longer filled with food. Rather, it held a small arsenal of handheld weapons, explosives, and cash from several countries. When Val said she'd stocked the safe house, she wasn't lying. The only thing she was missing was a rocket launcher. But with what he now knew about the woman, she probably had one of those hidden under the kitchen sink. The array of what she'd hidden in that cottage would have been unimaginable to him three days ago.

Three days. He walked beside Val into the lobby of the expensive hotel where they had a suite. That Guardian actually still employed him was a boon. Now the goal was to be of assistance instead of being a hindrance to the mission they'd been given. He wasn't some flashy double-oh-seven type. He was an enforcer. A rough man who'd used his power and brawn to intimidate and kill.

A bellhop ran toward him. "Sir, I'll take that for you."

Smith's grip held on the basket. "No, thank you."

The uniformed attendant blinked as if the words didn't register. Val smiled and placed her hand gently on the bellman's arm. "We're not done with what's inside. I'll call down when you can gather the basket."

Smith watched the man leave and followed Val into the elevator.

"That guy about had a heart attack. You don't know how intimidating you look, do you?" Val chuckled.

He slid his gaze to her. "I said thank you." It was better than a punch in the gut, which was his initial reaction when the man grabbed at the handle.

Val outright laughed at that. "True, you did."

She held up a hand in the suite, pulled out a slim pink cartridge, flipped it in some way, and started moving about the room. He saw the micro screen when she passed him. The technology wasn't lost on him. He knew she was scanning the room, but the thought of needing to check the room was something he wouldn't have considered.

He sat the heavy basket down and waited as she finished her sweep. "We're good," she said as she returned to the living area. "The courier should be here in about three hours. Let's get this unloaded and into our luggage."

He followed her into the bedroom and watched as she pulled two suitcases out of the closet. Her hands deftly found what she was looking for, and she pressed simultaneously along the top and the side. The suitcase's interior opened, displaying an area the length of the suitcase about three inches deep. She opened both sides of each suitcase. "Okay, half the money in one, half in the other. Even amounts for each country, that way, if we have to leave one suitcase, we'll have money. After the money is stacked, you can secure it with these straps." Val lifted the Velcro straps and put a stack of bills in one, securing it tightly. They worked quickly, securing all the money between the two cases. "Next, we secure the weapons. Hold on." Val jogged to the bathroom and came back with a can of hairspray.

She dropped the can on the bed. They positioned the weapons to ensure they fit and placed the det cord, explosive pins, and three small blocks of C4 into the vacant areas.

"How are we going to secure these?"

She smiled and winked at him. "Watch and learn."

Val took the top off the hairspray and shook the can. "Pick up the .45." She nodded to the gun in his bag. He lifted, and she sprayed the contents on the patch where he'd had the handgun. "Set it down."

Smith watched as the foam from the can blossomed around the weapon.

"It will harden and keep the weapon from shifting. It's non-reactive, so it's also safe to use with the explosives."

"Won't this be seen at any security checkpoint?"

"No. Check it out." She held up the flap. "This is called high-Z foam. It shields everything in here from X-ray."

"But when they see the X-ray is blocked, won't

they do a hand search and realize the luggage is too heavy?"

"That's what this is for." She lifted the cloth and showed him a light film. "This duplicates the appearance of translucency. I've never had a problem, and let's face it. Security going into Russia isn't that big of a deal. Getting *out* of Russia will be our issue."

Smith lifted each item as she pointed to them and then placed them back. When they were finished, the suitcases were lined with everything they'd loaded into the picnic basket. He glanced at his watch. "We have an hour." He hadn't realized the time that had passed as they worked.

"Let's get packed up. Once we run the table on the op, we'll probably be leaving." She put her hands on her hips. "Sorry about cutting the vacation short."

Smith moved to the closet where she'd placed his clothes. "I believe capturing Komal is more important."

Val stopped pulling her clothes from the dresser in the room. "We aren't capturing him."

He digested those words as he placed the clothes on the bed and started to fold his shirts exactly how he'd been taught in the military academy. He removed the hanger from another shirt and folded it, placing it carefully into the suitcase.

"Aren't you going to ask?" Val said as she placed her clothes in the suitcase.

"No." He knew exactly what her comment meant. He was internalizing once again being asked to take a life.

Her hand landed on his forearm, and he stilled. "Smith, if you can't or don't want to do this with me, tell me now. This is what I do. If we find Komal, he won't live to hurt anyone else. I will see to that personally."

He glanced at her hand. "I understand, and I haven't changed my mind. I'll go with you." He reached for another shirt to begin to fold it. His mind was a swirl of activity. Activity that hadn't been fine-tuned in years.

She pushed in front of him. "Don't do that. Tell me what's going on."

He stared at her for a moment before listing the things churning through his mind. He'd killed before. He'd never been caught. Suspected, yes. Any evidence that could be used against him? No. The killer he'd been in the past slowly awoke from several years of ... slumber. He slipped into his enforcer's role as one would slide on an old worn pair of jeans. There was no effort, and he, unfortunately, felt comfortable knowing what was required. “I’m considering the ramifications of killing a person on a train. It's a contained area, which means limited access and limited egress. I’m also thinking about the staff onboard. How do we walk off that train without anyone knowing we’re complicit? What are our emergency escape routes? How many men are guarding Komal? Will they be eliminated, or will they be a continued risk after we take him out? Where are his allies? Are they on the train? Are there others trying to do the same thing we are doing? Who is supporting Komal on his trip through Russia?”

A slow smile spread across Val’s face. “Mr. Young, I should warn you that intelligence like yours really turns me on.”

He blinked and then laughed. “I doubt it.”

She slid her hands up his arms. “Don’t. You are the most amazing man. Sexy and smart. A hell of a combination.”

Smith lowered his eyes, wishing she wouldn’t play with him like that. He wasn’t sexy. He was just … big. He would let her play her games with him because, in all honesty, he was incapable of denying the woman anything. But he knew all too well that at the end of the mission or when someone more suitable was found, he'd be cast off like the street trash he was. "We should finish packing. Perhaps there'll be time for us later."

She sighed as if she were put out. "Why do you have to make sense?"

"Because one of us must." He stepped to the side and took another shirt off its hanger. As they worked quietly, he internalized the need he'd developed for Val. The fondness that had somehow turned to more. He was a pathetic example of a man. He'd started to fall for a woman who only wanted a good time. A woman whose heart was buried with a man better than he'd ever become. A woman he'd known only a short time. He folded his slacks and jeans before placing them carefully into his suitcase. But he would have the memories of her, and perhaps through time, that would be enough. It was more than he had now.

Only moments after they'd finished packing, there was a knock at the door. Smith made his way to the entrance and opened the door, allowing Harbinger into the suite.

"I come bearing gifts." Harbinger lifted a canvas pouch in one hand and a takeout bag in the other. “Fish and chips. You’ll have to ring up room service for the beer.”

Smith took the bag of food he was offered and sat it down on the table after securing the door behind Harbinger. He looked inside the bag. “There are four meals here.”

“Yup. We have one more joining us. He’ll be along shortly.” Harbinger tossed the beige canvas bag onto the couch. “Looks like things are heating up for us.” He walked over and kissed Val on the cheek. “Hope you’ve been being good.”

“Am I ever?” Val purred the response and laughed when Harbinger swatted her on the ass. Smith clamped his jaw down.

A twinge of absolutely misplaced jealousy shot through him. Instead of allowing anyone to see his reaction, he pulled the meals out of the plastic bag, then went to the phone to push the button for room service. “What do you want to drink?”

“Wine,” Val said immediately. “An oaky Chardonnay.”

“Beer. Stout if they have it,” Harbinger added.

Smith ordered the drinks, forgoing any alcohol for himself. His mind was already muddled with his blooming infatuation for Val and the resurgence of things he’d wished he’d never have to think about again. He listened as Val and Harbinger chatted like life-long friends. Not inserting himself into the conversation, he stood by the table, realizing he'd adopted the posture he'd used for years. His hands clasped loosely in front of him, and his head lowered. He was once again in the service of others. *That* he knew. *That* was his life. The interlude between the end of Simmons and the evil associations the bastard had maintained and the death of Mrs. Henshaw had been just that—an interlude.

"Hey, come sit with us." He lifted his head at Val's voice. Before he could say anything, a knock sounded at the door. Smith once again made the trek to open the door.

He blinked and looked out the peephole again, opening the door wide. "Well, how the hell are you doing, old friend?" Smoke, or Dan Collins as he first knew the man, clasped him on the arm and strutted into the room. Smith shut the door and watched Val hug the newest arrival. Harbinger gave Smoke a hug, and they laughed about something said between them.

Val waited until they were done and popped the question on Smithson's mind, too. "What are you doing here?"

"I'm here to run the table. Archangel wants no mistakes or questions. If we need to, we'll call in, but everyone wants to keep this between as few people as possible. You look weird as a brunette, by the way. Have you swept the room?"

Val crossed her arms and lifted an eyebrow. "I look good no matter what hair color I have, and no, I didn't feel like it." She threw up her hands. "Of course, I swept the room. What an asinine question. We're clear."

"Man, you are always so touchy. Where's the pouch?" Smoke looked around.

"Over here. Dinner is on the table. We've ordered up some beer and wine." Harbinger filled Smoke in.

"Good. We'll wait for the drinks and tackle what's in this packet. Smithson, how are you enjoying London?"

Smith smiled politely, knowing he'd never share his thoughts about the events that had transpired since they'd landed in England. So he hedged, "They drive on the wrong side of the road."

Smoke laughed and once again clapped him on the arm. "You get used to it. The first time I was here, I almost had a heart attack. I made a right-hand turn and went into the wrong lane. A little old lady driving a Fiat stopped as I careened to the other side of the road. I still remember her shaking her fist at me and screaming obscenities that a nice little gray-haired grandma shouldn't ever say." Smoke laughed. "I had enough explosives in the trunk of that car to blow half of London to the moon. Believe me, I remembered real quick what side of the road to drive on from then on. It was one of those life-altering moments."

Smith opened the door when the beer and wine arrived, tipped the server, then shut and locked the door. After Val scanned the buckets chilling the alcohol, they broke out the food and gathered around the table. Smoke took a bite of fish, then rubbed his hands together. "Why can't we duplicate that in the States? So damn good." He opened the pouch and dropped a folder onto the table. "Okay, on to business. Here's the gist of the operation we've built. This is Komal. Here with a beard and different colored hair. Here clean shaven, here with a hat on. His chief of security is believed to be this man, Vosser Blanton. He escaped custody after initially being arrested with Komal. Where Blanton is, Komal won't be far behind." Smoke placed several pictures on the table. Blanton carrying what looked like a machine gun, his face distorted in a yell. "These were taken by surveillance cameras at the Hague."

Smith leaned in and studied the pictures. He committed both faces to memory.

"Val, you and Smithson are going in as a married couple. Mr. and Mrs. Smithson Dimitri Young."

Smith almost broke his neck, jerking his attention from the pictures to Dan. "What? Why?"

"Duplicity, I'm afraid." Smoke stared straight at him. "Not only are you a citizen of Russia by birth, but you're a member of Bratva royalty. We don't disguise the fact that you are in the country, and if by chance you are stopped or detained by anyone, your mother's maiden name is a get-out-of-jail-free card. At a bare minimum, it will delay any action and allow you to extricate yourself from any sticky situation you find yourself in."

Val put her hand on his thigh under the table. He didn't react to what he assumed was meant to be a comforting touch. "Then we'll give him a fresh start with a new alias when we return to the States, right? The Russian mafia will come looking for him if we use them, especially if they find out they were used to do work for our government."

"That's already underway. My friend, you will have a fresh start after this mission. A new name and no connection to your past." Smoke looked at him expectantly.

Smith stared at him for a moment as he processed that information. "And if I choose to leave Guardian after this mission?"

Val's head whipped in his direction, but she didn't say a word. Smoke pursed his lips and nodded. "The alias is yours, although we'd like you to stay with us."

"Why?" It was the only question that mattered.

"Personally, because I know what type of man you are. I know Guardian needs men of integrity and honor. You have both of those qualities. But I'm not going to blow smoke up your skirt. This mission is the only thing you must commit to, and that alias is yours. Free and clear. If you want to walk away after this mission, that's your call. But I think you'll like working for the good guys better than working for your past employers."

Smith nodded, acknowledging everything Smoke had said, and he couldn't help noticing that Val's hand slid from his thigh.

Smoke reached into the canvas bag. "Alternate passports." He handed one to Smith and the other to Val. "American if you need them. Keep them under metal foam until you do." He reached into the bag again, retrieving two reddish-maroon-colored passports with a double-headed eagle emblazoned in gold on the cover. "Russian passports. You're flying from Heathrow into St. Petersburg. Honeymooners on the way home from a trip to France. The computer trail of those trips will activate when these passports are scanned. We've wiped Smithson's image from the New York to Heathrow trip and his passport scan, so the story will sync up if anyone looks. We don't anticipate they will, at least not from the Russian side. There's a small airfield seventy kilometers east, northeast of St. Petersburg." Smoke pointed to a location on the map. "A car will pick you up at the airport and deliver you. A small aircraft will be waiting for you, and the pilot will fly you to Novosibirsk to visit your wife's sick mother. We've used the pilot and his wife, who will pick you up, before, and they've been paid handsomely, but we're not fools. While on that plane, you will mention your mother and her maiden name in casual conversation. *That* will ensure the silence that the money we're pumping into this operation might not guarantee. Nobody wants to cross the

Solntesevskaya family, especially people being paid by unknown entities. And it will enforce the allusion we've built with this pilot that we're connected to the highest levels in the country. Your reservation has been made at this hotel. Paid in full through the date the train will travel through Novosibirsk. Public transportation is available at the airport where you'll be taken."

Smith couldn't fault the logic, but that didn't mean he liked it. Val glanced over at him. She would be the only one who would understand his silence. Smoke ate a french fry or chip, as they called them in London. Harbinger was demolishing his take-out while Val thumbed through her passport. He glanced down and read the passport. Valerie Young. He pushed his food away, his appetite lost. His small world had exploded, and the shreds of his past were once again haunting him. Would he ever be free of it?

Smoke wiped his hands and reached back into the canvas bag. "Here are your rings. Smithson, I took a wild-ass guess at what size you wore. If it doesn't fit, no big deal. We know Val's will." He tossed Smith a small black box. Inside, on one side, was a diamond the size of a dime and a gold and diamond band. Val plucked them out of the black velvet.

"Rather ostentatious, isn't it?" She slid both rings on her left hand. "Here." She took the thick diamond and gold band from the other side and slipped it on his finger. It was snug, but it fit. "There you go, hubby." She leaned up and kissed him on the cheek. "Until mission do us part."

Harbinger and Smoke laughed and went back to eating while Smith stared at the ring. *Yes. All of this is temporary, isn't it?* He closed the box and handed it back to Dan. That was as close to being married as he'd ever get. Instead of lingering on that thought, he asked, "What's our exit strategy?" He had no concerns for himself. The future wasn't his focus. It hadn't been in a long time. He lived exactly one day at a time, but Val needed a future. She needed an exit strategy, and she needed him to do his part in this mission. He'd do it to the best of his abilities.

Smoke took the box and tossed it back into the canvas bag. He flipped the map over and pointed. "These are the three routes the train can take. There's only one passenger train scheduled, so if Komal is going by train, he will be on it. From Moscow, all trains run on a common rail to this point, eight kilometers past Irkutsk. Here the train goes to Beijing via Naushki or continues to Chita, then drops through Zabaikalsk and down to Beijing. Your only option is to force the train to go through Skovorodino and the rest of the towns to Vladivostok. Here. We'll have water transport waiting for you. Questions?"

"Updates and communications?" Val looked at him.

"CCS suggested old school computer email dead drop right under their noses. Draft emails they can't monitor. Komal is the baby. If he's on the trip, we'll leave a message that the baby is on the way. If he's located elsewhere, it was false labor."

Smith looked at the email provider that Smoke pointed to. "Do you have an account?"

Val shook her head. "I will. Is CCS setting it up?"

"Yes, with your standard password. The email address is the usual before the government's designation."

"No AOL or Gmail in Russia?" Harbinger laughed.

"They have it, but they also monitor it. This system is archaic. CCS says it's our best bet. So find an internet café or check in if you can get internet on your phone. If nothing is in the draft folder, there are no new updates on your mission."

Smith sat and listened to the people around him. The intricacy of the plan was astonishing. The people behind the scenes had worked hard to make the mission successful. Having support and knowing that Komal was a criminal who had committed atrocities focused this effort, unlike anything he'd participated in before.

Val stared at the map and traced the route they wanted the train to take with her manicured fingernail. "Are we sure the train is supposed to go to Beijing? There's a chance it could go to the sea."

"We believe it was supposed to travel to China. The Russian railway system isn't centrally computerized. Each node is separate; from what CCS can tell, most are on standalone computers. She'd need a staff of a hundred or a supercomputer to find or verify the route information in time to help. Unfortunately, at the moment, neither of those is a fully operational asset. Hell, you two could be going on a vacation courtesy of Guardian. We just don't know."

"Where do I fit in?" Harbinger asked.

"You're heading to Mongolia and meeting up with Oscar Team. There, you'll be on-site to switch the rails and provide backup. If Komal is on the train, Val and Smith, you'll need to have a signal displayed outside the train. Something Harbinger and his team can't miss. When you see it, you switch those tracks and then jump on board as the train heads to Skovorodino and on to Vladivostok."

"I've never worked with a team before." Harbinger leaned back in his chair. "What exactly is my role?"

"You'll be the lead, and Alpha has made sure the team leader understands that fact. You and the team's communications specialist know Russian. It will have to do. You and that team *are* the exit strategy. The train will take an additional time to reach Vladivostok if it doesn't stop at any of the towns along the way. When it doesn't, someone may raise the alarm. That's where the team comes into play." Smoke withdrew a packet and handed it to Harbinger. "Your passport and money. You'll fly to Kazakhstan and meet with the team at the airport. Together, you'll travel to Mongolia. The borders aren't guarded except at the roadways."

"How will we get into Mongolia, then?" Harbinger took the envelope and zipped it into his jacket pocket.

"Horseback over the border and then find

faster transportation. Oscar Team has been working in the Kazakhstan and Mongolia areas for years. They know how to get you where you need to go."

Harbinger rolled his eyes. "I hate horses."

"Why?" Val asked. "They're such regal creatures."

Harbinger shook his head. "Dogs are regal creatures. Horses are huge and can kill you."

Smoke laughed. "Dude, suck it up. Any questions? Concerns? Anything we overlooked? Now's the time to put it out there."

Smith glanced from Val to Harbinger, then to Dan. When there was nothing from them, Smoke leaned back in his chair. "All right. Harbinger, you have an hour to make it to Heathrow."

"Not a problem. I'm packed, and my kit is in the car." He stood as did everyone else. Harbinger shook Dan's hand, then Smith's, and finally hugged Val. "I'll see you in Mongolia." The man gave them a two-finger salute and walked out the door.

"You have three hours before you need to be at Heathrow. Oh. I almost forgot. Here's your earpiece, Val. You still have one, right?" Smoke turned to look at Smith as Val popped her communications device in her ear. He nodded. He hadn't taken it out. "Good. Do you mind if I have another one of those stouts before I grab a taxi back to the airport?"

Val laughed and went to get him a beer while Smith excused himself. He needed a moment to internalize everything he'd just heard and witnessed. He made his way into the bathroom and sat down on the edge of the tub, breaking down the mission in his way. One, there was no proof Komal would be on the train. Conjecture only. Two, Guardian was using his mother's name to solidify or perhaps maintain a network they had in Russia. That her name was useful was the only good thing to come from her in a long time. Third, they'd have help in the extraction. Fourth and most important, his time with Val was temporary, and he needed to keep that in mind. She would be acting, and he would have to force himself to remember that. A part to be played now that the vacation jaunt she'd wanted was a thing of the past.

"He's fine. He processes everything in minute detail, and you already know he isn't the most talkative man in the world." Val's voice in his ear was shocking after not hearing it for a few days. Smoke must have asked about him. He stood and moved to the bathroom door.

"So, you really want to go there?" The warning in Val's voice was real as she responded to something Smith couldn't hear. He grasped the door handle, a protective roar flooding through him. He turned the knob.

"No. He doesn't know, and I won't tell him."

Smith froze with his hand on the knob. *Know what?*

He could hear Smoke talking through the door of the hotel room. The low rumble of a masculine voice was audible, but he couldn't hear *what* Smoke was saying. "He's not ready. Not yet. Given time, I think it may work, but if it doesn't, well, then, this trip was all for naught, wasn't it?"

He dropped his eyes to the handle of the bathroom door. *So, this is what? An experiment? He wasn't ready for what? Joining Guardian? Killing? Being used ... his parents. Of course.* He turned and leaned against the door. *Of course.* Why else would Guardian want someone like him? He wasn't the important factor; Guardian's end plan was something to do with his family. *God, that made sense.* Why else would they keep tabs on him? Why else would someone like Val pay attention to him? All the dots suddenly aligned into a straight and cohesive concept. He tilted his head and maneuvered the small device out of his ear. She was with him to make sure he complied.

He stared at the earpiece and felt his resolve and his disdain grow. He didn't care if Guardian used him somehow to manipulate his mother's connection to the Bratva. That wasn't what hurt. As the warmth of the blossoming infatuation he'd held for Val drained, it was replaced by anger. He'd sworn he'd never be used again. Yet there he stood embroidered into a tapestry of Guardian's weaving.

He looked up at the ceiling. Komal needed to die. He used children. Children should have their innocence and childhood, not be harvested for war and sex. For that reason alone, he'd complete the mission. Then he'd walk away when the team left for safe waters. He'd learned to survive on the streets of New York. He could learn to survive in Russia.

He placed the earpiece on the top shelf of the bathroom and opened the door. Time to show Guardian that he wasn't the man they knew as Mrs. Henshaw's keeper.

12

Val poured a glass of wine and sat down across from Smoke. He'd become the entire class' mentor since Demos retired. Smoke was a big brother to all of them, whereas Demos was the father some of them had never had.

"Is the big guy okay?" Smoke took a drink of his beer.

Val glanced to the bathroom and smiled. "He's fine. He processes everything in minute detail, and you know he isn't the most talkative man in the world."

"When are you going to tell him that you really like him? Don't think I didn't notice what you've been up to." Smoke fell back against the back of the couch. "I've known you for years, and I see it, even though you don't want anyone to know. You care for him deeply."

"So, you really want to go there?" Val narrowed her eyes at Smoke, but he was right. She'd grown to care for Smith in a way she hadn't cared for anyone since she'd met her late husband. Smith was completely different. Her attraction to him didn't make sense, but since when did matters of the heart actually make sense? "No. He doesn't know, and I won't tell him." She needed him to be focused on the mission. She had the experience and knew that even though they had passports and means to complete the mission, eyes would be on them. It was dangerous going into Russia. Moreso doing what they planned to do.

"You're making a mistake. This guy is literal, Val. He's never experienced love from anyone except maybe Mrs. Henshaw. Don't fuck around with this. Tell him how you feel."

She shook her head. They'd made progress, but ... "He's not ready. Not yet. Given time, I think it may work, but if it doesn't, well, then, this trip was all for naught, wasn't it?"

"Cynical doesn't look good on you, sweetie.

Don't play this guy like you would a mark. He's real, and he's vulnerable." Smoke stood up. "I've got to dart, or I'll miss my return flight."

Val stood and hugged her friend. "Take care of yourself," she whispered in his ear.

"I always do. You think about what I've said." He gave her a final squeeze.

"I always do," she repeated his words. "Whatever it takes."

"As long as it takes." Smoke kissed her on the cheek. "Seriously, you look weird as a brunette."

She rolled her eyes. "I'm changing back to blonde. CCS sanitized Heathrow, right?"

"They did." Smoke looked past her. "Hey, Smithson. I'm on my way back to D.C.," he said, then moved toward the door. Val spun and watched as the men shook hands and said goodbye. An odd feeling that something wasn't quite right with Smith zapped through her, but he didn't act any differently. When Smoke left, he locked the doors and headed into the bedroom.

"What are you doing?" she asked, following him.

He went into the bathroom and reached up to the top shelf. "Putting in my earpiece."

"Good idea. I need to change, and then we'll

head to the airport." She watched him as he threw a glance in her direction. He simply nodded, and she got that feeling again. "Smith, are you all right?"

He stopped and turned toward her. "I'm fine. I'm concentrating on the mission."

"Okay. Do you have any questions or concerns?"

"None." He moved out to the living room, and she watched him pick up the Scotch bottle she'd ordered the first night. He poured two fingers and walked to the window. Turning to look over his shoulder at her, he said, "I thought you were going to change?"

"Yeah, I'm going to take a shower. Can I convince you to join me?" She'd love to have one-on-one time with him before the mission started.

He shook his head while looking out the window. "I need to think."

She blinked at the response feeling rebuffed and ... hurt. "All right." She went into the bathroom and removed her wig and contact lenses. The color pallet for her foundation, blush, and eyeshadow looked garish against her nearly white hair and blue eyes. She stepped into the shower and let the warm water surround her. After her shower, she became herself—well, as close to herself as she'd ever been—and dressed. When she emerged from the bedroom, Smith was standing in front of the window, the glass of scotch still in his hand. She flicked her gaze to the scotch bottle. The contents hadn't diminished. She walked up behind him and placed her hand on his back. "Is everything all right?"

He blinked and looked down at her. "Perfect." She watched him glance at the clock. "I'll get my jacket. Call for an attendant for the bags?"

Worry crept through her. She'd known him long enough to know that was not the norm. "No. You need to tell me what's changed tonight. What happened?"

He turned and looked at her and repeated the words she'd said to Smoke, "He's fine. He processes everything in minute detail, and you know he isn't the most talkative man in the world." He paused and quoted her again. "So, you really want to go there? That's what you said. What don't I know, Val? What won't you tell me? Why am I not ready? What's going to take time? Guardian using me? Guardian using my parents? I asked you if this was all a game to you. You denied it, and I believed you. I. Believed. You."

"What?" She turned toward the bedroom and then the bathroom. "You heard?"

He sneered at her. "I heard."

She moved forward and placed her hand on Smithson. "Not all of it."

He whipped her hand off by flinging his arm out. "Enough."

"Oh, *hell* no." Val moved and grabbed his hand, spinning and bringing it up in leveraged hold behind his back.

Smith had skills and strength. He broke the hold and walked into the bedroom. *All right, you asked for it, mister.* Val slipped out of her heels and sprinted toward him. He heard her coming and turned, which was just what she wanted. She launched and wrapped around him, scissoring her legs around his neck and pulling him back onto the bed. Val scrambled, using his momentary shock to lock her arm and put him in a chokehold.

Shit! What? Val hung on tight. The man had a strength she'd never experienced and stood with her still locked around his neck and spun, trying to grab her. "Stop it, damn it! You're not ready to hear that I care about you. I don't want to scare you off, and Smoke didn't have any right to go there!"

Smith grabbed her leg and jerked her. He lifted her foot as she fell from his back, giving her an angle. She reached between his legs, grabbed his quad, and kicked free of his grip on her leg. Landing on her knees, she pushed up, lifted his leg, then lunged to her feet, sending him sprawling to the floor. The thud of his weight hitting the floor reverberated in the room. Val hustled. She moved on top of him, panting for breath, her knees pinning his shoulders and her hands holding his up over his head. She stared down at him. "I care about you, you asshole! That was what we were fucking talking about. That's the whole damn secret. If this trip didn't work out and you don't care for me after we're done, then that was why the whole trip would be for naught. Damn it, you don't believe anyone can care about you, and I want to prove I do."

Smith stared up at her breathing just as heavily as she was. He moved so quickly that Val didn't see it coming. They rolled, and he was on top of her. She went limp. "You're a big, muscled hunk of nothing but heart, and you've been hurt so many times by so many people. You don't trust me."

He stared at her. "You don't trust me."

"I do. I think I have since I saw how you cared for Mrs. Henshaw. I'm telling you the truth. There's no game. The only thing I want is you." She stared up at him. Those dark eyes bored into her, and she gazed up at him, letting him see the absolute truth.

A loud pounding on the door turned both of their heads. "Hotel security!"

"Kiss me, now," Val said to him.

Smith dropped his weight between her legs as she wrapped her arms around his neck. When security opened the door, they broke the kiss. Smithson's brow lowered. "Can I help you?"

"Ah, ma'am, is everything okay? We got a complaint from the people below you saying they heard shouting and things falling?"

Val laughed. "The suitcase fell off the bed, and I was shouting with delight because my husband was taking me on a surprise trip." She lifted a finger and turned Smith's face, so he was looking at her. She sighed. "Close the door on your way out, please."

The side of Smith's lip ticked up, and he dropped for another kiss. Val heard the man leave the room but didn't break the kiss. When Smith finally lifted, he stared at her. "I don't understand how you could care for me."

"And that is why I didn't tell you. I wanted to share experiences to show you that I did. I know how badly you've been treated. I don't play games, Smith. I don't tell people I care for them if I don't."

He stared at her for a moment. "You hit me with a flying leg scissor."

"Well, you deserved it." She scrunched her nose. "You're stronger than I thought. Use that the next time we're in bed together."

He rolled his hips, and she felt the ridge of his cock against her. "Oh, so now we know a bit of sparring is foreplay." She laughed as his face turned red. "That's okay. It got my engine revved, too."

He laughed and looked up, his face immediately falling. "We need to go. We'll be late for the airport."

Val tipped her head back and looked at the digital clock. She groaned. "To be continued." She lifted and kissed him. "You call for the car and the attendant. I need to fix my hair.

Smith stood and offered her a hand up. When she was on her feet, he cocked his head. "Smoke was right."

She smoothed out her clothes and adjusted her belt. “About what?”

“You do look weird as a brunette. I like this much better.” He lifted her hair in his hand, and she smiled and spun, heading to the bathroom. Maybe she put a little extra sway into her walk as she went. Smith was an enigma, and if she had her way, he’d be hers.

13

Smith handed his passport to the old, bored-looking security guard at the St. Petersburg airport. The man flipped the page open to his picture, looked at the passport, and then at Smith. Flipping through the passport, he looked at the stamps in the back of the book, then he closed it and tossed it to Smith. Well, so much for worrying about the passport being looked at critically. Val stepped next to him and presented her passport, smiling at the guard. The older man did a double take and looked at her ring and then at Smith. "Your husband?" the man grunted at her.

She looked up at him. "Yes. We're returning from our honeymoon in France."

The man narrowed his eyes and glanced between them again. Smith leveled a stare at him that could melt cement. The guard shrugged, flicked her passport back to her, and called, "Next."

"What was that all about?" Val whispered as she put their passports into her purse.

"He didn't believe you would marry me." It was pretty obvious to him.

Val snorted an indelicate laugh. "Whatever." They claimed their luggage and wheeled them to the street. Over the crowd, Smith saw an older woman holding a sign with his name on it, and he angled Val in her direction. Once they reached the woman, who stood in front of an old Spetsteh all-terrain vehicle that had been driven hard, he loaded the suitcases in the trunk. Then as Smith climbed into the front seat, Val sat in the back.

The older woman got into the truck and merged into traffic. She reached down to the floorboard and brought up a bucket. "Pampushka." She took off the towel and grabbed something wrapped in wax paper, handing it back to Val. "Kiefer." She nodded to the midsection, and he lifted the door. He took out two small plastic bottles. He opened both and handed one to Val. Grabbing a small pampushka that was split and buttered, he took a sip of the Kiefer and ate the bread. His mother had always told him never to eat dry bread and gave him this food for a snack between meals. He watched out the window as they traveled away from the city. He'd love to explore St. Petersburg, but that wasn't on the agenda.

Not another word was muttered the entire trip. Val's eyes were closed when he turned back to check on her, though he doubted she was asleep. Still, he followed her cue, rested his head against the old, cracked headrest, and watched the country go by. It was beautiful and heart-wrenching at the same time. They drove through small villages where skinny dogs lay in patches of shade and old women were outside washing clothes. Whitewashed homes sometimes displayed colored shutters, but more often than not, the structures were unadorned. There were few power lines. He kept his head and eyes forward, not wanting the woman driving to notice him taking in everything. He assumed the conditions wouldn't be new or shocking for a person who was supposed to be from the country.

Smith had researched Russia. He wanted to know about his mother's homeland. What he'd found was a life of strife for most citizens. A duality was seen in most major countries, but not to that extreme. Those in power, the ones who lined their pockets instead of providing for the general population, lived in the lap of luxury. Those who didn't worked from sunup to sundown and beyond to survive. The farther east they traveled, the harder survival would become. Vast areas of Siberia didn't have regular power, and the native inhabitants lived on what the land provided.

He turned to look out at the countryside, but his mind traveled back to the hotel room. Val had literally flown through the air to take him down. He wasn't expecting it. He allowed himself a happy smile. Tough and beautiful. Val had dropped him, not once, but twice. Few people had done that. Of course, he'd never fought a woman before.

He thought of the women he'd been ordered to kill. Memories that would haunt him forever. He made sure it was quick and, if possible, without their knowledge. The men he'd killed were monsters. Not on the level of evil he was currently hunting, but those hits didn't bother him as much.

As the woman turned down a bumpy gravel road, Val sat up and looked around. They drove a little farther, and a structure came into sight. A hanger, Smith assumed.

The woman pulled up next to the building and shut off the old vehicle. "Go there. He's waiting." She pointed to the door, got out of the truck, and trudged to the small house on the other side of the larger building.

Smith got out at the same time as Val. "I'll grab the luggage." Russian was the language from there on out. She nodded and stood near him, but he could tell she was keeping an eye open. When they had their luggage, he led the way through the door, flipping his sunglasses up to see the darkened interior.

"Good. You're here. Come, we need to go now." A small man, about sixty-five, stood and waved them over to a small Cessna. "One bag here." He pointed to a storage compartment. "One bag goes here. I have to keep the weight balanced."

He looked at Smith, then at Val. "You on the passenger side. Her behind me." He grabbed a foam pad. "No seat." He handed the pad to Val, who lifted her eyebrow at his retreating back.

"No seat," she said in Russian. "Oh, fun."

Smith chuckled. "At least he gave you a cushion."

She turned her attention to him. “Guess what I’m thinking.”

Smith tried hard to stop the smile that spread across his face. “I wouldn’t want to hazard a guess.”

“See, I told you, you *are* extremely intelligent.” She lifted the foam pad mimicking the pilot. “No seat.” She walked to the plane where the pilot waited with the door open.

He followed her and gave her his hand to help her to the step and into the tiny aircraft's back storage area.

He waited until she was settled before walking around the plane and getting in on the passenger side. The pilot tossed them both headsets and put his on. Then he started the engine and tapped on several dials on the dash before he grunted and moved the plane to taxi to the end of the dirt runway. He glanced back at Val. “Comfortable?”

He heard her reply in the headset, so he knew the pilot heard her, too. “I’m telling your mother,” Val said with a pout.

He laughed at her because she was batting her eyelashes at him. “My mother wouldn’t believe you. Nadia Solntesevskaya always flies first class. This was the quickest transportation my grandfather could arrange to get you to Novosibirsk to see your mother."

The pilot's reaction would have been funny if he wasn't the one in control of the aircraft. His jerk was as sharp as if someone had stabbed him. He did a double-take at Smith. If there was a family resemblance, Smith wasn't aware of the fact, but the man seemed to go a bit pale.

"Are you all right?" Smith asked. The guy had better not pass out as they sped down the runway. The pilot seemed to catch himself and turned back to the business at hand. He pulled back, sending the aircraft into the air.

The flight was low, which he assumed would keep them below any radar in the area. Either that or the old plane couldn't fly any higher. He'd wager on the latter. The drone of the aircraft stifled any conversation, even with the headsets. The pilot pointed to the horizon as dusk was covering the land. "Novosibirsk."

Some time later, they landed in almost pitch dark, although there were landing lights on the runway. The little plane touched the ground with several large bumps and hops, and once it had stopped, Smith was grateful for the ability to get out and stretch. The pilot solicitously helped Val out of the plane, unlike when they took off. He raced around the plane and attempted to unload one of the suitcases, tugging the handle to lift the case over the small lip. Smith reached over the smaller man and easily lifted it out of the compartment.

The pilot all but bowed to them as they left. He hailed a cab, and they slid into the back seat after securing the luggage. "My back is killing me." She leaned forward and rubbed the small of her back.

"Too many gymnastics earlier." He chuckled and turned so he could rub her back for her. She groaned and lifted her light jacket.

"Just a bit lower, and the gymnastics were your fault," she hissed when his thumbs moved over a knot in her muscles. He worked the area carefully, trying to loosen the tense muscles. In fact, their fight wasn't the cause. More than likely, the awkward curled position she'd been sitting in for hours while they flew to Novosibirsk caused the knots. Val sighed and leaned back into him. "I'm tired."

He was, too. The lack of sleep was catching up with him. "We'll sleep well tonight." He kissed the top of her head, and his eyes met the taxi driver's as the guy glanced back. The driver smiled and turned on the blinker, merging into city traffic.

Forty-five minutes later, with the shades drawn in the small but clean room at the hotel Guardian had booked for them, he watched Val sweep the room. She pointed to the phone and then to the electronics she held in her hand. A red dot appeared on the screen. She continued around the room and pointed to the light switch. Two electronic devices detected. She put the device away and pulled him into the bathroom, turning on the water. She whispered, "Probably installed when the hotel was built. They have power, or the scan wouldn't have detected them. I doubt they're being monitored, but we need to stay in character."

"No problem. The clerk gave you a code to sign into the internet. Do you want to check for any updates?" he whispered before she turned off the water. He wanted to know if there was any further information on Komal. She held up her finger, went to the bedroom where they'd left the luggage, and retrieved her phone from her purse.

Smith watched over her shoulder as she typed in the password for the hotel wi-fi. Her thumbs flew over the keyboard as she searched for the email platform and entered her login and password. There was no draft message. "Nothing yet." She shook her head. "We'll keep checking." She signed out of the email website.

"Let's get dinner and then get some sleep." Val yawned and shook her head. "I could use about eight hours of uninterrupted rest."

"Perfect." He picked up her purse and handed it to her. "Let's go."

Smith shut the door behind them, but Val stopped him. She glanced both ways down the small hallway and pulled a single strand of hair from her head. She wet her lips and pulled the strand across them, then draped one end across the doorknob and pressed the other against the door jamb. The hair stayed where she placed it. She smiled at him and slid her hand through the crook of his elbow. "If someone goes into the room, we'll know."

"What if it just ... unsticks?" he asked as they approached the stairwell.

"Then it'll still be on the door handle. If someone turns the handle, the hair will fall. Simple."

He nodded. Her knowledge was superior to his, yet she called him intelligent.

They asked the clerk behind the front desk for

recommendations for dinner. She suggested two places. They chose the closer of the two, so they could walk. God knew he'd sat enough, and Val seemed to agree.

The restaurant was nicely furnished, and they were seated at a semi-private table. "Order for me?" Val smiled at him and put her hand on his arm. He knew it was part of the charade. Val was a woman who made up her own mind. He examined the menu, which wasn't extensive. When the server stopped at the table, he ordered. "We'll have the Potemkin Soup, followed by the Zhizhig-galnash."

"Excellent. And for the third course?" the server asked.

"Tea and Muraveynik cake." He handed the server the menu and turned back to Val.

"I've had the soup, and Zhizhig-galnash is meat and gnocchi. What is Maraveynik cake?"

"My mother made it for Christmas. It is a funnel cake with nuts and condensed milk. One of the few good memories I have of my time with them."

Val laid her hand over his. "Then I'm sure I'll love it."

He listened as Val chatted about a scarf she saw

in a shop and loved. If anyone were to listen in on the conversation, there would be nothing unusual about the couple in the corner. He answered at the appropriate time and laughed when she did. Val was a natural at the art of deception. They ate hardy food and finished it with tea and the chocolate confection of his childhood. Val's eyes rolled when she tasted the cake. "So good!" Neither of them left a scrap on the plate.

They leisurely strolled back to the hotel. He took off his suit jacket when Val shivered and draped it around her shoulders. The wind was brisk, but he didn't care. She smiled and toed up to kiss him. "Thank you."

She put her arm through his, and they continued the stroll. "When we get on the train, I'll have to do whatever I need to get to Komal." She looked up at him. "Whatever I have to do."

He stopped and stared down at her. "Why are you telling me this?"

"I ... hell. I don't want you to think I enjoy it. I don't. I do what I do for one reason only. I come on to them to separate the monsters I hunt from the pack they run with and kill them."

He narrowed his eyes. "I will kill the pack. You kill the monster."

"When it's done, we'll have our vacation."

He put his arm around her and started them to the hotel. "I don't need a vacation with you to know I care for you."

She leaned into him. "Then take me back to the room and show me."

14

Val woke when a door down the hall shut. The noise wasn't loud, but it was distinct from the subtle noises of their room. The door at the end of the hall opened and closed, and she heard the faint fall of feet going down the stairs. Relaxing, she continued to listen for anything that suggested hostile intent. When there was nothing, she pushed her hair away from her face and lifted her cell phone. Almost six in the morning. Smith sighed and rolled over onto his side, facing her. She smiled at the memories of last night. The sex was always great, but last night, there was something more than just sex. There was a connection, a type of reverence that usurped the physical desires. He cared for her. In Smith speak, that was huge.

She cared for him, too. The thought was painful and liberating. Painful because she thought she'd never care for anyone again. Liberating because she knew it was time. Time to let go of the past and move on. Val closed her eyes and thought of her late husband. *I will always love you, but I need this. I need him. He's a wonderful man.* Val knew it was time to move on, and she'd go forward with Smithson.

"Why are you awake?" Smith mumbled in her ear. Even half asleep, he'd remembered to speak in Russian.

"We slept for seven hours." She reached for her phone and logged in now that the light wouldn't wake her sleeping partner.

"Bright." Smith rolled onto his face.

She chuckled and signed into the email account. There was a message, and she read it. "Come on. We have to get up, showered, eat breakfast and make it to the train depot by ten." She tapped him on the shoulder, and he lifted his head, squinting at the cell phone screen.

He read the screen and dropped back down

into the pillow. “It doesn’t take me four hours to get ready.”

“Fine, you sleep. I’ll shower.” She slipped out of bed and went into the bathroom, where she turned on the shower and placed her cell phone on the sink. Komal was either seen on the train, or they suspected he was now on board.

She let the warm water pour over her. According to the information in the packet, Komal was a narcissistic bastard. She knew exactly how to play on that particular brand of crazy. The unknowns for the mission, though, were legion. She knew Smith would have her back, and thankfully, she didn’t have to worry about Komal’s chief of security. She’d make sure Smith knew Vossar Blanton was his to eliminate before they boarded. There would be others, for certain. Val washed her hair and worked through what would give them the best chance of survival and escape. She’d have to ensure she was alone with Komal before they hit the switching station. She’d kill him, and then she and Smithson would need to take out whatever contingent, Russian guards, personal bodyguards, or loyalists would hinder their escape. Phones would be a problem if there were reception in the area. Cell coverage could be obtained if not in the rural areas as they passed through towns.

Val felt the cool air as Smith opened the bathroom door. He pulled the shower curtain back, and Val couldn't help the smile that crossed her face. His hair stood up in a cacophony of directions, and his morning stubble would take most men a week to grow. "It's too small for both of us."

"I'm done." Val stepped out of the spray and reached for a towel. Smithson moved sideways, and they changed positions. She stood beside him and towel-dried her hair. With the water running, they could talk quietly. "Blanton is yours. Keep him away from the target and me. We'll make our move the night before we meet with Harbinger and the team. By that time, we'll have identified all his entourage."

He nodded. "The rest of the security team may have to be eliminated."

"Acceptable. Civilian casualties are not. But if it's the only way to eliminate our targets, we do what we must do." She wrapped her towel around her body and reached for her comb. "We'll need to figure out how and when to separate Komal from his pack.

He cocked his head at her and nodded. “We’ll think of something.”

“Good. Now, soap up and get a move on. We don’t want to be late.” Val closed the shower curtain. Smithson whipped it open again and grabbed her, pulling her toward him. He dropped a kiss on her lips. “Good morning.”

Shocked, she laughed, “Well, good morning to you, too.” Smith shut the curtain again, and she shook her head. The man was an enigma, to be sure.

~

VAL EXTENDED her hand to the conductor as she stepped into the luxury coach. “Welcome. Your tickets please?”

Val turned around. “My husband has them.”

Smith stepped into the coach and removed the tickets from the inside pocket of his jacket. “Very good. We have your accommodations ready.” He lifted his hand, and a young woman in black slacks and a red vest stepped forward. “Daria will show you the way. Your luggage will be delivered to your quarters.”

Daria greeted them. “This is the bar car. Cocktails are served in the dining car also." They moved from one car to the next. "This is the dining car. Meals are at eight, noon, and six. We have full-time kitchen staff, but room service is not offered. Seating is open." They walked into another richly appointed car. "Here we have the game car. The gentlemen have a self-serve whiskey bar here, and we have supplies for card games. Wagers are illegal." Daria smiled. "If we find out about them." She laughed and led them out the door and to the next car. "Next, we have two sleeping cars. You will be in this one." They entered another car, and Daria escorted them to their room. "We will convert the seats into beds while you are at dinner." She looked at Smithson. "I think you may be cramped, sir."

Smith glanced at the small seats and shrugged. "I'll be fine."

"Your luggage is already here. Your private shower is through this door. Once you empty your luggage, please let us know, and we will store what you don't need."

"What are the other cars up there?" Val asked, wide-eyed, pointing out the window.

"The first is the kitchen car. Above that is a supply car. We can carry enough food and water for three round trips, if necessary, but always refill when we stop in Moscow. Then the luggage storage car is after that. Next is staff lodging. Beyond that are the coal car and the engine."

"So, all the guests are in these two cars? That's amazing."

"Normally, we have more passenger cars, supply, and staff cars." Daria shook her head. "The schedule and number of cars always change."

"Thank you so much for the tour." Val gave the woman a few rubles before she stepped into the compartment and shut the door behind her. Smithson handed her the scanning device, and she conducted a quick sweep. "Nothing, and you will be a pretzel by morning." She waved at the small red crushed-velvet benches that would be their beds.

Smith sat down on one and leaned into the corner. He put his feet on the cushion across the small aisle and crossed his arms. "I've slept in alleyways and behind dumpsters. This is good enough for me."

Val sat next to him and stretched out, putting her feet on his legs since they wouldn't reach the other side of the compartment. "Can I tell you again how much I think your parents are troglodytes?"

His laughter under her ear was a precious sound. "You like that word."

She chuckled and shrugged. "I do. It has a ring to it, doesn't it? I learned it from a friend, who you'll meet one of these days. His name is Flack. He called his sister Trisha's in-laws that. I had to look it up. Don't tell him."

"Your secret is safe with me."

The horn on the train blew plaintively. "We'll be moving soon."

"When we do, we'll remove our guns but keep them hidden and stash most of the money where we can access it. We'll need cash to buy favors and silence if we need to improvise and leave the train." Val snuggled against him. "Besides, I have what I need right here." She lifted her shoe and twisted her ankle to show him her prized possession.

"Black shoes with high heels. I can see how that could kill someone. A heel through the eye." Smith poked fun at her.

"Well, close, but a little different than you think. Don't judge a book by its cover." She crossed her leg and twisted the heel at the rubber heel guard. A long, pointed, thick needle slid out. "I have these installed in every set of high heels I own." Val held it up in the air and turned it around. "Strong enough to go through the ear into the brain if you shove it just right. But normally, I use the eye. Bigger hole in the skull."

He took the small base of her heel and examined the needle. "How do you get close enough to shove this in his eye without them suspecting it?"

She twisted to look up at him. "It's an acquired skill."

She saw the moment her words hit pay dirt. He didn't say anything for several moments. Then he asked, "You've used this before?"

She took it back and slid the needle back into its home, twisting the rubber heel guard to lock it into place. "Carbon steel and titanium alloy. Strong enough to go through bone. And yes, I've used it many times. There is very little, if any, struggling afterward. Effective, efficient, and usually silent." There'd been an occasion when she'd had to break a neck to silence a target. She hated that cracking sound. It sent shivers down her spine, so she avoided using that tactic if possible.

"How many assignments have you been on for Guardian?"

She looked back at him. "Does it matter?"

He gazed at her and shook his head. "It doesn't. I'm sorry for asking."

"Don't be. I do the work I'm assigned. Maybe once or twice a year, I'm given an assignment or a support role to assist one of the others. Other than that, most of my time is spent alone or training."

"Living a solitary life is difficult at times."

She turned so she could see him better. "It's difficult all the time."

The train jerked forward, and Val lurched closer to him. He wrapped his arms around her and dropped a kiss on her lips. "Time to get to work, Mrs. Young."

Val exited the room after retrieving their personal sidearms. Her Beretta PX4 Storm weighed less than two pounds, was slightly over five inches long, and held eleven 9-millimeter rounds. Ten in the magazine and one in the chamber. It sat comfortably in the purse she carried. For the rest of the day, they planned on getting the lay of the train and the individual cars. Things like where the roof hatches were located and if there were any floor hatches would be valuable to know. Additionally, they needed to assess the passengers and, if possible, find Komal.

Val made her way back to the bar car. Several people were lounging by the windows, and she chose a seat away from them and made herself comfortable.

"Would madame like a drink?"

She smiled at the waiter and ordered a Chardonnay. After the waiter delivered it, she sipped the wine and examined the bar car. Two ways in and two ways out. There was a roof hatch in the middle of the car. It was centered between two chandeliers and trimmed with crown molding, but it was available if needed.

"May I sit?" a woman about sixty asked and pointed to the chair across from Val.

"Of course." She smiled at the woman and resumed her examination of the bar car.

"You must have gotten on in Novosibirsk. I don't believe I've seen you before."

Val blinked back to the woman across from her. "We did, yes. My husband and I decided to extend our honeymoon. When we found out tickets were available, we couldn't resist."

The woman tilted her head. "Congratulations. My husband and I are celebrating our fortieth wedding anniversary. I've always wanted to ride this train. My father told stories of the grand cars and the pampered service. We boarded in Moscow, and I'm looking forward to seeing some of the less populated areas. Are you traveling all the way to Beijing?"

"Yes, we are. Are you?"

"Yes. There really isn't any other place that will do, is there? These villages are ... less than adequate."

"Perhaps." Val didn't like the woman. She seemed entitled and snotty.

"I wouldn't have chosen this as my honey-moon." The woman shrugged.

"I look forward to having my husband to myself." Val chuckled and lifted her wine glass.

"He works hard, spends time away? All men seem to do this at times." The woman was a talker, wasn't she?

Val nodded, smiling sadly. "He works very hard." Taking care of Mrs. Henshaw had been a labor of love for Smith, and no one would tell her differently. She'd seen how he'd been with her when she'd visited. She'd always been interested in him. He was the type of man she naturally gravi-tated toward and watching him care for the old woman sealed the deal for her. She'd had a soft spot for the man for as long as she'd known him.

That spot had become fertile, and her fondness for him had grown. Smoke hadn't been oblivious to what she was doing, but then again, Smoke saw more than most people knew. He used that sense of humor to mask how observant he really was.

"Dear?"

Val blinked and looked across the aisle at the other woman. "I beg your pardon; I was lost in thought." Val smiled sweetly.

The woman smiled knowingly. "Of course. I said my name is Nadia."

"Valerie." She extended her hand and shook the other woman's.

"An American name?"

"I believe it's British. My mother enjoyed literature and named me after a character in a story she enjoyed." Val pushed the question off with a laugh.

"Mrs. Young." The railcar steward came up to their conversation area.

Val and Nadia turned at the same time.

"Yes?" Nadia spoke, smiling at the server.

Val's eyes popped wide. Thank God no one was looking at her, or she hadn't answered first.

"We're getting more lemons from the kitchen car. Your cocktail will be ready shortly."

"Thank you." Nadia nodded and turned back to Val.

"I learned to love a vodka martini with a lemon twist while living in America." She shrugged. "Not many good things come out of America, but I'll make an exception for a lemon martini." The woman laughed, and so did Val, although her heart was racing like a thoroughbred stallion. There was no way the woman was Smith's mother. Dear God, she needed to excuse herself and find Smith. What if he ran into his father?

15

Smith built a map of the train in his mind. They'd agreed to meet in the dining room for dinner, so he didn't expect to see Val barreling toward him as he opened the game car's door. She pushed him backward and closed the door behind him. "Turn around. Go back to the room. Hurry."

He could sense the urgency in her tone even if the earbud weren't in place. He opened the door for her and shut it behind himself. "What's wrong?"

"I think I just met your freaking mother!" She threw her hands up in the air. Smith tried to make sense of what she said, but it was impossible. "I'm not going insane. Stop looking at me like that!" Val paced as far as the little room would allow her. "Holy hell. It can't be."

"Wait, Val. Why do you think this woman you were talking to is my mother?"

"Her name is Nadia Young. She lived in America, and she loves martinis, but the waiter had to send someone to the kitchen car to get—"

"Lemons," he finished for her.

She dropped her hands from her hips. "They're going all the way to Beijing. You can stay here. I can do the rest. You could have motion sickness or something." She started pacing again. He put his hand on her shoulder and turned her. "It has been over twenty years since they've seen me. I am physically three times the size I was when I left. My nose has been broken four times, and my jaw once. Life has changed me. They won't recognize me."

"A mother will always recognize her children." Val shook her head. "God, what are we going to do? I have to hit the damn target. We can't bail off the train at the next town." She twisted out from under his hand, walked the two steps to the other side of the car, and returned. "You'll have to stay in here."

Smith shook his head. "No. They won't recognize me. I was ... much different."

"How so?"

"I was an insecure, shy young man. I wouldn't meet people's eyes. I was terrified of my own shadow. Life on the streets strengthened me and taught me to fight for what's mine. I'm not that child who desperately wanted to be anywhere but in that home."

Val stared up at him. "And if they recognize you?"

Was her concern for him or the mission? Probably both. He pushed a bit of her hair that had fallen to her cheek. The moment's intimacy was special to him, even with the stress of having his parents on board. "We laugh and claim I must be a doppelganger."

"And the names on our tickets?"

"Did you look at the tickets?"

"No."

"There are no names, only quarter numbers. I only gave my name to the ticket agent to retrieve the tickets. I haven't told anyone my name, have you?"

"No. Just my first name."

"Our passports haven't been asked for. There's no security on this train, and it probably won't be until the border with China. We are Russians who are traveling in Russia.

Val grabbed his arm. "Are you sure you can handle possibly seeing your parents? You heard my side of the conversation with your mother, right."

"I did. You sounded pleasant, and yes, I'm positive." He pulled her into his arms. "Everything will go on as scheduled."

"Don't." She pushed away. "I don't need comforting. I need to figure this kink in the plan out."

Smith sighed and crossed his arms over his chest. "I wasn't holding you to comfort you. I was holding you because I wanted to and thought I could."

Val stopped. She dropped her head back between her shoulder blades. "Ugh." When she straightened, she looked at him. "Okay. I'm sorry. That was a snap judgment on my part. You can hug me whenever you want as long as we aren't actively working on a case. I have to let Guardian know they're here."

Smith lifted an eyebrow. "I can deal with that. How will you tell Guardian?"

Val grabbed her phone. “Damn it. There’s no internet.”

“Then we ignore them and do the job we were sent to do. Have you seen Komal or Blanton?”

“No. It seems like everyone is taking an afternoon nap or something.” She shook her head. “I was going to ask Daria if she’d get permission to take me on a tour of the rest of the train.”

“Great idea. I’ll go with you if they allow it. Until then, I’m going to play cards and have a drink. Hopefully, one or more of our targets will show their faces.” Smithson pulled down the sleeve of his cashmere jacket she’d had tailor-made for him. “My wife has good taste.”

“She damn sure does. Oh, wait.” She grabbed him. “What name should I call you?”

He shrugged. “Ivan Medvedev?”

“Okay.” She turned and paced back and forth a bit more. “This is what I’ve been thinking. Komal is a narcissist. He has to be the best, have the best, and be seen as the best. If he ever comes out of hiding, you need to one-up him in small things. Give him a reason, several reasons. He’ll look for a way to be better than you.”

“All right. I don’t see the connection.” He could irritate the man, but to what end?

"I've trapped men like this before. He'll go after me. He'll seduce me or maybe take me by force. That's when I'll kill him."

"By force?" No, he wouldn't let that happen

"Relax. I'll let him think he has control, then turn the tables. I've done this before. Don't doubt my skills."

He didn't like it. "You'll let me know if you're in trouble?" He tapped his ear.

"You'll know, now kiss me like you mean it, Ivan. I have to go make myself irresistible."

Smith pulled her into him and kissed her. "You already are." The sweet taste of her was intoxicating. He broke the kiss and waited for her to open her eyes. When she did, he told her the truth that lay in his heart, "You make me crave things I've never allowed myself to think possible."

Val reached up and laid her hand on his chest. "Allow yourself to believe it's possible—with me."

He smiled down at her. "I'm trying."

"I know." She stepped away. "Go play your games. If you see him, one up him. Nothing major, just several little things." She went into the bathroom and closed the door. Smith took a deep breath and left the cabin. When he once again got to the game car, he was ready for whomever he'd meet.

There was a game in progress in the corner. He walked to the bar and dropped a single ice cube into a tumbler. Then he examined the offerings and chose a Scotch. He casually drifted over to the table and watched as they played. Poker. Five-card draw. He couldn't see any cards; everyone kept them face down after glancing momentarily at them after the deal. He watched them ante up. Those who remained threw in the cards and were dealt the same number.

Smith could tell who was going to win. The man on his left. There was a predatory look in his eye as he sized up his opponents. The larger stack of chips in front of him gave him a massive advantage. He would win because he could buy the pots by outbidding the others. Even if the others went all in and won, the man would still hold an advantage.

He went to another vacant table and took a new deck of cards out of the box. He shuffled them and laid them down for a game of solitaire. He heard the door to the railroad car open and close but didn't look up. He pretended to be lost in his game. Being too interested in the comings and goings of others would only draw attention to him. Attention they didn't need.

"Excuse me, do you speak English?"

Smith looked up into the eyes of Vosser Blanton. "A little." It was the common answer when someone asked if someone spoke another language.

"Would you like to play?" Blanton dropped a stack of rubles onto the table.

"What game?" He reached back to his wallet and pulled out an equal size stack of bills.

Blanton smiled and sat down. "Do you know seven card stud?"

"I have heard of it, yes." Smith loved the game. He was good at poker because he remembered what cards had been played and knew the probability of a good hand versus those of a shit hand.

Blanton got up and went to the bar, leaving his stack of money on the table. Smith took another sip of his scotch and waited for Blanton to return.

When he did, the man sat across from him. "I have friends on the train, and I expect they'll be here soon. We'll wait for them. We can take their money instead of each other's." The man laughed at his joke and saluted Smith with his freshly poured drink.

"Would you actually be their friend, then?" Smithson asked, leaning back and taking a drink of his Scotch.

"To you, yes. To them? Maybe not today." Again, the man laughed. He extended his hand. "Name's Vosser."

Smith reached over and shook the man's hand with a strong, firm grip. Blanton was a dick and tried to squeeze harder. Smith stopped the contest with a pressure that could easily break the man's hand and sneered. "I think maybe you try too hard." Blanton released his grip, letting his hand go slack, and Smith followed suit, releasing Blanton's hand and leaning back, staring at the man.

Smith lived his life as an enforcer. He knew when he was being sized up. Perhaps it was Blanton's job to get a feel for new people on the train.

Blanton shook his hand. "Strong as a bull."

Smith snorted. "No. Strong, period." He wouldn't let Blanton marginalize him.

"True." Blanton agreed before he took a drink.

"What do you do, Mr. ... I'm sorry, I didn't get your name."

"Ivan. Ivan Medvedev." He took another drink of his scotch.

"Ivan. Good Russian name. What do you do, Ivan?"

Smith put his drink down and leaned forward on his forearms staring directly at Blanton. "I mind my own business."

Blanton blinked and narrowed his eyes. "That's always a good thing."

Smith swept his hands over the cards on the table and collected them. "In business, in life, and in general." He agreed with Blanton and shuffled the cards. A laugh from the other table broke the silence. Smith didn't turn around. "The man wearing the black shirt won."

Blanton slid his gaze that way and then lifted his eyebrows. "It seems he did. How did you know?"

His gaze moved toward Blanton for a moment, still shuffling the deck. "He had the most money when I sat down."

"Frequently when gambling, money changes hands very quickly." Blanton took a drink.

"That's why you never bet more than you can afford to lose."

"True. Ah, here are my friends." Blanton motioned over three men. Smith glanced up and then dropped his eyes. Val started talking to Daria in his ear, so he had to concentrate on what was happening in front of him. "Ivan, this is James, Melvin, and Sam."

He placed the deck of cards on the table and stood, extending his hand to his father. "Nice to meet you, James." He shook Komal's hand. "Melvin." Turning to the last man, he offered his hand. "Sam." He spoke in English.

His father blinked and stared at him. "Have we met?"

Smith stared back at his father. "I don't believe so. Why do you ask?" He sat down, as did the rest of the men.

"You look familiar. Like someone I used to know." His father switched to Russian.

Smith lifted an eyebrow. "Is that a good or a bad thing?" He answered in Russian.

"What are you talking about?" Melvin interrupted.

Smith turned to the man who had hurt an untold number of children and translated what they'd said word for word. He didn't know if Komal or the others spoke Russian, but if he did, he wouldn't give them any reason for concern.

"Shall we play?" Komal said. "Seven card stud. Where are the chips?" He turned and motioned for the man with the black shirt. "Buy in?" Smith watched as the man with the black shirt divided the chips equally among the players and placed the money in the chip box. He handed Blanton the cards and watched as he shuffled and Komal cut. The hand was dealt, and all the players settled the pot.

"Have you spotted Komal and Blanton?" Val asked the question. *How in the hell was he supposed to answer that?* He didn't respond or speak until it was his turn to bet. "I call."

"If you're with them, raise on the next bet. Ten for each you've identified."

He watched the cards, and when it was his turn, he tossed in four chips. "I raise forty."

Blanton swiveled his head. "Are you working on a royal flush?"

Smith wasn't. The hearts in his hand didn't match the spades on the table, nor did the numeration make a straight. He shrugged. "Pay to see."

All but Komal folded. The murderer sneered. "I think you're bluffing."

Smith turned a bored look toward the murderer. "Then pay to see."

Komal stared at him for a long moment. The railway car door opened again, and Blanton did a double take. "There you are," Val said as she entered his peripheral vision, but he didn't look up at her, even when she stood beside him and put her arm around his shoulder. He continued to hold Komal's stare. The man broke and threw in his cards. Only then did Smith look up at her. Val had her hair swept up, dangling in places, and she'd changed clothes. The tight, low-cut, almost see-through blue dress she wore matched her eyes and the jewels she'd put on. She purred, "Darling, don't take all their money, and don't forget dinner is in an hour."

He reached up and pulled her down for a kiss. "I won't forget. Go, do lady things, and let us continue our game."

Val trailed her finger along his lips in an intimate gesture before turning her gaze to the other men at the table. If he'd ever seen a study in lust, that was it. He saw the lecherous stares of the men at the table. His father included. Val smiled to let all of them know she knew exactly what they were thinking and turned. All eyes except his followed her out the door.

"Your girlfriend?" Sam asked.

"My wife," Smith corrected him. "Deal the cards, or are you going to eye-fuck my wife some more? Believe me, she's out of your league and off limits."

James cleared his throat. "She's a beautiful woman." Sam and Blanton agreed, and all but Komal had the grace to look like kids caught with their hands in the cookie jar. The game continued until a rail car steward walked through the car playing dinner chimes. Smith had won several hands but lost enough that the others were still in the hunt. He could cat and mouse the players all night if he needed to do so.

"We hold the table and continue after dinner?" James suggested, standing. "My wife wouldn't be pleased to dine alone."

Smith stood also. "I agree." He glanced down at his chips and turned to leave the car.

Komal waved them toward the dining car. "Enjoy."

James hesitated. "You aren't eating?"

"In a moment."

Smith heard the dismissal as he was walking away. He entered the dining car and found Val sitting with his mother. *Of course.* The table where they were was set for eight. He made his way to the table and paid his mother absolutely no attention until he bent down and kissed Val. "I'm on time, as requested."

She laughed and leaned into him once he was seated. "Nadia, this is my husband, Ivan."

His mother extended her hand. "It is a pleasure to meet you, Ivan."

He lifted a bit from the chair and kissed his mother's hand. "And you."

"Oh, you have a true gentleman." His mother smiled sweetly. She lifted her empty martini glass and smiled at James as he approached the table. "This is my husband, James. He's American, but I love him anyway."

The waiter showed up with another martini and took away the empty glass.

"How many martinis have you had today, my dear?" The sarcastic drawl of his father's question couldn't be missed.

Nadia lifted an eyebrow. "Obviously, not enough." She turned back to Val. "As I was saying, my youngest daughter married very well to a businessman in Moscow. My oldest daughter is married to the chairman of the State Duma."

"The chairman? Isn't he ... older?" Val truly looked confused.

"A price one pays to be in the correct family."

Nadia waved Val off and turned her attention to Smith. "Ivan, what is it that you do?"

The slight slur in his mother's question indicated her martinis were just as important now as they had been when he was growing up. "I don't do anything." Smith lifted his finger for the server.

His mother blinked. And looked at him. "You know, you look like …" She turned her head to her husband. "He looks a little like Smith, doesn't he?"

"I thought so, yes." James nodded.

"Family money on my mother's side allows me to invest, and I do quite well in the Asian markets." He interrupted their conversation and ordered a glass of Scotch for himself and a Chardonnay for Val.

"Ah, so we meet again." Komal, flanked by Sam and Blanton, strode up to the table.

His mother muttered something under her breath, and his father gave her a sharp look. "We didn't meet earlier. I'm Melvin, this is Vosser, and this is Sam." Melvin introduced himself to Val.

"We were just discussing Ivan's lack of work," James said and laughed.

"Oh?" Melvin said as he draped his napkin over his lap.

"He's an investor in the Asian market." James continued.

Melvin smiled and nodded. "Capitalism makes the world go around."

"I disagree. Powerful men make the world go around, but capitalism does assist in purchasing comforts for us," Smith corrected the man. Everyone except Komal laughed. Val smiled at Smith, and a knowing look passed between them. Smith had put himself above Komal. It was a calculated slight and one, as Val had reminded him, Komal wouldn't tolerate. Komal's eyes slid to Val, who was now chatting with his mother.

Smith took his drink off the server's silver tray after Val reached for hers and listened to the banal conversations in the room and at the table. If Val had guessed correctly, Komal would want to take him down a notch to prove his delusions of grandeur. Val believed she would be the way Komal would do it. Smith took another sip of his scotch and slid his gaze to Komal, who was staring at him. Smith dismissed him with a roll of his eyes and scanned the rail car as if he were a king and the passengers his minions.

16

If she could have stood up and cheered, she would have. Smith had baited Komal with the aplomb of a seasoned veteran in her profession. She didn't doubt he'd handed the man other subtle snubs while they were playing cards. The stare-down she'd witnessed when she floated through the railroad car and displayed all her assets to the crowd was intense, and Smith had won. His story about his mother's assets and the Asian market was perfect. Although the more Nadia drank, the more she stared at Smith. Val kept redirecting her attention until the first course arrived.

Val looked up while eating her soup to catch Komal staring at her. She blinked and flashed him a friendly smile, acting oblivious to the game being played between the two men. He returned her smile and nodded. "Have you ever worked as a model?" He asked across the table.

She laughed. "Goodness, no, I like to eat."

Smith leaned back and put his arm on the back of her chair possessively. She smiled at him and then looked back at Komal. "What do you do?"

Every person at the table stopped eating. Val looked from person to person. "Did I put my foot in it? Are you famous?"

Komal chuckled, and the tension at the table seemed to melt a bit. "Famous? No," he demurred. "I am just a man." He spread his hands out and smiled.

Nadia snorted and tossed off the rest of her martini. She lifted the glass and caught the attention of the server. "Are you enjoying the train ride?" Komal asked Val.

"I am! It's so exciting. Ivan thinks I'm silly, but I adore trains. I always have. He didn't want to be so far from his markets and internet, but I love the beauty of the countryside." She animated her talk and had everyone's attention. "Oh, Ivan, Daria said she'd see if I could get permission to go farther up and see the other cars."

"You shouldn't bother the staff." Smith reprimanded her and took another drink of his scotch.

"Oh. I'm sorry," Val said, shrinking in on herself.

"I could take you on a tour. I have access to whatever I want," Komal suggested.

"You do?" She turned to look at Smith. "Would it be all right?"

"I'm sure our new friend has better things to do with his time." He stared at Komal.

Komal shook his head and said, "Not at all. I'd be honored, and the offer stands." The next course was served, and through the rest of the dinner, she sent a couple of glances Komal's way and nervously smiled when she caught his eye.

She'd set herself up as bait, but Smith had truly set the trap. Komal was everything his psychological profile said he was. After dessert, she and Nadia excused themselves. She helped Nadia to her quarters before returning to her cabin. As a routine, she swept the room and then got ready for bed with the earpiece in. She listened to Smithson as he called, folded, and raised. He didn't engage in small talk, so the game must have become serious. The main lights outside the cabin had long ago dimmed when

Smithson returned to the room. He smelled of cigars and scotch.

"You won," she said into the darkness.

He chuckled. "I did. I didn't mean to wake you."

"I wasn't sleeping. How badly did Komal hate losing to you?"

"He was not pleased. Yet, he was bluffing. The cards to beat my hand had already been dealt. I went all in, forcing him to put up or shut up. He isn't that good of a player. I think the others lost to him on purpose."

She heard him take off his clothes and then feel his way to the small bed on the other side of the little aisle. "Your mother doesn't like him. She called him a few select words and warned me to stay away from him when I escorted her to her room."

"My mother is a miserable judge of character, but in this, I'd have to agree with her." He yawned. "If I'd met him on the street, I would have avoided him. He's dangerous."

"So are his guards."

He made a humming noise of agreement. "There are three I've seen. Sam, Blanton, and a man in a black shirt were in the game car. Mr. No

Name lurks, and he's someone to watch. I'll point him out to you tomorrow."

"We have two full days to get through. I suggest we avoid them by staying in our coach for tomorrow. Let him stew. The next day, we'll reel in the fish."

"How?"

"I'm not sure, but when it happens, we'll know." She sighed and turned on her side. "Three men. You're good taking care of all of them?"

Smith was silent for a long time before he answered. "I have no problem killing. Their skillset could be better than mine, but I have my size and strength as an advantage."

She nodded into the darkness. The car rocking against the rails of the track provided a repetitious and soothing tune. "You were magnificent in the dining car tonight."

"And you were beyond beautiful. I wanted to dig out their eyes for how they lusted after you. Even my father was entranced."

"And yet none of them can have me. Only you." She sighed deeply. "Sleep well, Smith."

"Good night, Val." He moved, presumably to get more comfortable. She closed her eyes and listened to the wheels clacking against the rails. They'd set the trap, now to entice the rat.

VAL STRETCHED and rolled into Smith's chest. They'd spent the day finding inventive positions to have sex in the railway car. Turning down the service to put the beds away and not leaving the car to eat either breakfast or lunch had given them plenty of time to experiment. She glanced at the time on her cell phone. "We need to dress for dinner, and I'm hungry." Still, she didn't move, and his big hand on her back kept stroking the skin up and down her spine.

"What is the plan for tonight?" Smith's voice rumbled under her ear.

"Let's go early enough to get a table for two. I want to face Komal. We'll eat, then go into the bar car for drinks. That should allow him to make contact."

"How do you know he will?"

"I don't. But if he follows character, he won't be able to resist poking the bear."

"I'm the bear."

"My bear." She patted his chest and nodded.

"Just be above it, above him. Subtle, but above. You've already bested him at gambling and in a group conversation. Doing so again tonight will intensify his resolve to better you. Maybe a poker game after dinner tomorrow night? I'll suggest he take me on a tour while you play." She'd kill the bastard. The rail car stewards wouldn't come to make up the room until morning. If she killed him in his quarters, they'd find him, but that's when Harbinger and his team would switch the tracks and come aboard. Timing was everything.

"All right." Smith agreed. She smiled against his chest. Any other person would have a hundred questions, work against doubt, and postulate what-if scenarios. Not Smithson. He was one in a million, and he was hers.

"We should get dressed," he said after about five minutes.

"We should," she agreed but didn't move. "Can I tell you a secret?"

He chuckled. "I've told you all of mine."

"All of them?" She tipped her head back to look at him. His eyes narrowed, and then he waved his head. "Most of them."

She laughed. "That's why I'm falling for you,

Smith. You're unlike anyone I've ever met before. I'm in pretty deep with you. Pretty darn deep."

He lifted a handful of her hair and let it trickle through his fingers onto her back. "You're not alone." He met her gaze. "And for the first time in my life, I'm not either."

She lifted to kiss him. It was soft, lingering, and full of the words neither of them was ready to say. It was a promise of things yet to come.

THEY WERE among the first in the dining car and chose a table where she could face where the others had been seated the night before. The game car was occupied, but Smith hurried her through the aisle as they'd discussed. She looked around as they exited the car and gave a friendly wave toward the men she'd met the night before. Gullible was a pretense she wore well.

They both ordered drinks and held hands, talking as the car slowly filled. Komal and his men took their usual seats, and she had a direct line of sight to him. "So far, so good," she whispered to Smith.

"Ivan, would you and your lovely wife care to

join us for dinner?" It seemed James had been elected to extend the invitation.

Smith stood, towering over his father. He shook the man's hand. "Thank you, no. We've already been served. He pointed to the soup the waiter was placing before them. "Join us for drinks in the bar car afterward, perhaps?" he offered.

"Of course. That sounds good." His father smiled at her before returning to his table. Val waved at Nadia. The woman smiled and lifted her martini glass. Val shifted her gaze. Komal nodded his head, and she demurred, smiling. Smith leaned to his side, blocking Komal's view of her. She popped her eyes up to look at him. "Oh, that was a good move."

His lip ticked up for a second. "We should eat. It appears we'll be drinking tonight."

She spooned up the soup and a bite of bread. "Remember, give me time with him. Hover, but not too close."

He chuckled. "Your exactness is enchanting."

She blinked, then laughed at him. "You know what I mean."

"I do. But I like to hear you laugh," he admitted. They were one of the first to finish their meal, and Smith helped her stand. Her dress was a high cowl neck in the front. The back was a drop to the base of her spine where the cowl rested. His hand landed firmly on the middle of her bare back, then slipped to her ass. She looked over her shoulder and waved to Nadia, glancing again at Komal. Yes, she definitely had his attention.

Smith ordered them drinks, and they secured several small standing tables in the corner of the room that would allow them to circulate and talk. Nadia was the first into the bar car, and the bartender lifted a hand in acknowledgment when she asked for the usual. "I didn't see you at all today. I was horribly bored," Nadia said as she stood next to Val. "I'm glad you didn't get the tables with the chairs. I have been doing nothing but sitting all day." Nadia glanced around. "These people are boring, and my husband's acquaintances are not people I choose to associate with."

"I'm sorry. We decided to have some time alone." Val leaned against Smith. "He's the most wonderful man I know, and I was selfish today." She looked up at him and hoped he knew it was the truth even though they'd contrived the time together to further the mission.

He stared down at her, and the barest hint of a smile curled his lips. Nadia made a swooning sound. "Love. It's a wonderful thing that makes people do the most insane things." She took her martini from the waiter and drank half of it. "Bring me another, please," she said, catching the man before he went too far.

Still holding the glass, she stared at Smithson. "You look so much like him."

"Who?" Val asked.

"A boy I once knew." She stared at her martini. "A long time ago."

Smith tightened next to her, and she put her arm around his waist. "They say we all have ... what are they called?" She looked up at him.

"Doppelgangers," he replied.

Val laughed. "That's it. Such a silly word."

"Rather like troglodytes," Smith said as she took a sip of her wine. Val sputtered and coughed after inhaling the wine rather than drinking it. She grabbed the napkin someone pushed in front of her and tried to control her coughing. She barely managed and looked up at him. "That was not fair."

A brilliant smile spread across his face. "But I do love to hear your laughter."

She rolled her eyes. "Don't make me choke, then."

Nadia downed the rest of her drink. "A personal joke, I take it?"

"Yes, sorry," Smith said. "Let me refresh your drink. Nadia, may I hurry your martini along?"

"Will you? Thank you so much." Smith headed to the bar, which was starting to become busy as people finished dinner. Val moved to where he had been standing, allowing someone to stand between her and Nadia. James was the first to appear. He headed straight for the bar and stood beside Smith. Komal, Blanton, and Sam entered next. Blanton and Sam scanned the crowd, assessed the situation, and headed toward the bar. Komal walked toward them.

"Ladies, it seems the gentlemen have left you unattended."

Nadia rolled her eyes. "And look what they let in the door."

Komal smiled politely, but the look he gave Smith's mother would have flayed her skin in one fell swoop if it had been possible. Nadia huffed. "I'm going to find that drink."

"She's had a few." Val chuckled.

"She lives in a bottle." Komal's disdain for Nadia was as clear as Nadia's disdain for him.

He turned away from the bar and leaned on

the table, blocking her view of Smith, as a smile that Val assumed he thought was sexy spread across his face. "I've cleared it with the train staff, and I can take you on a private tour anytime."

Val popped her eyes wide. "You can?" She peeked around Komal's shoulder at Smith, who was on the way back. Blanton stopped him with a question, but she couldn't pay attention to their conversation now. She shook her head. "Ivan wouldn't like it."

"So don't tell him. It'll be our little secret."

She drew her brows together. "But how? The only time he's not with me is when he's playing poker. No. I'm afraid I can't."

"If I were to fix it, so he's playing poker. Say, tomorrow afternoon?" Komal leaned closer. "It would be our secret, and it would be fun."

She peeked around his shoulder. "Tomorrow after dinner. I can meet you at the end of the passenger cars. What time?"

"Nine thirty."

Val reached out and touched Komal's suit jacket. "Okay. But you can't tell him, or he'll be really mad."

Komal stared at her for a moment. "I look forward to it."

"You look forward to what, exactly?" Smith sat her wine glass in front of him, forcing her to step over to be closer to him to reach it. Komal smiled at the move.

"I told your wife how much I'd look forward to winning my money back. Would you consider a rematch tomorrow night? After dinner?" Komal baited Smith.

"If you wish to lose more money, who am I to decline?" Smith dropped his arm over her shoulder and took a drink of his scotch. She flashed a quick smile at Komal, hiding it behind her wine glass. Komal lifted his eyebrows a couple of times. The rat had sniffed the bait. Now to make sure the snap of the trap killed the bastard.

17

Smith sat down at the poker table. Komal, Blanton, Sam, and the man he hadn't named sat at the table with him. James had begged off with a headache, although he was fine at dinner.

"I'm in the room. I'm prepared, and I've checked my equipment. I know how to handle this guy. Don't let anything you hear break your character. You start to get worried about a half hour after Komal excuses himself or quicker if he makes a move on me. I'll let you know where I am. They'll follow you when you excuse yourself."

He didn't need the recap. Perhaps Val was nervous? More than likely, she wanted to make sure he wasn't. Killing wasn't hard. He had no problem taking Komal's guards out. The game's object would be to do it where no one would see them. The storage car or the luggage car was where he believed Komal would try to seduce Val. The only thing he cared about was her getting the job done without being touched by that slimy bastard. He knew she would play her part, but that didn't stop his stomach from turning at the thought of Komal's mouth on Val or his hands on her body.

"Shall we deal?" Sam asked, and Blanton cut the cards. Smith played using every advantage he had, but he won hands he shouldn't have. They were throwing games to him, keeping him in the game, no doubt. By the time nine-thirty rolled around, everyone was low on chips, and his stack had multiplied.

"I need to take a comfort break. Continue to play. I'll be back," Komal said.

Smith cocked his head. "That's not how the game is played. If you break, we all break."

Val's voice came across his earpiece. "He's leaving. I got it. Heading out now."

Komal shook his head and smiled. "My friend, you'll soon have all our money. Take theirs first, and I'll be back in time for you to take mine. Besides, we make up the rules on this train. Who is to tell us any different?"

Smith leaned back in his chair and stared at Komal, narrowing his eyes suspiciously at the man. Finally, he nodded. "Deal the cards."

~

Val didn't change clothes. She wanted that bastard Komal hot and bothered. She paced at the last door to the sleeping compartments and glanced at her watch, acting nervous and impatient. When he opened the door to the sleeping car, she smiled widely. She laughed as he approached. "I feel like a student who didn't go to class, but I want to see the rest of the train."

Komal's eyes raked over her, and she blinked, moving her arms across her chest, giving him the scared rabbit look. "Maybe this was a mistake." She moved against the wall to slide past him.

"No. No one will ever know. Come, I'll show you the train. It's magnificent and will be an experience you'll never forget." He opened the door and placed a firm hand on her back. She looked down the hall and stepped out of the car through the transition and into the next car. Komal nodded at the kitchen staff. There weren't any surprised looks on the kitchen staff's faces when he moved through the car.

They moved to the next in line. "The supply car," he said as they moved farther along the car.

"Oh, this is where they keep all of Nadia's lemons." She laughed and moved over to a bin holding beets and potatoes.

"Come. There's more to see." Komal moved through the car, barely giving her time to look around.

"Are you worried Ivan will come looking for me?" She jogged a little to keep up with the man.

"Your husband has been taken care of. I'm not worried about him at all." Komal opened the door at the end of the car and motioned for her to go through.

"Taken care of? Do you mean at the poker table? He's very good, you know." She moved through the outdoor transition to the luggage car and listened to Smith as he called on a hand. Komal shut the door, and she heard the slam of the deadbolt as it toggled into place. Val spun. "Why did you lock the door? Is this the luggage car?" She let Smithson know where she was. "I think I've seen enough. I should get back."

Komal grabbed her and almost jerked her off her feet. His hands dug into her upper arms. Val let him slam her into the door that he'd locked. "Stop it. What are you doing?" She struggled a bit, playing the part.

"You know what I'm doing. You want me. Why else would you have agreed to meet me?" He grabbed her thigh and dragged his hand up to her crotch, forcing her to spread her legs. "Stop it. No! Stop!" She struggled harder. Komal clamped his mouth over hers and pinned her to the door with his body. Using one hand to hold her hands above her head, he unzipped his pants with the other.

Val used her high heel to slam into his toes. He hissed and did exactly what she'd hoped he'd do. He threw her to the floor and sat on top of her. He ripped her dress from her neck to her waist. "Stop! No!"

"Shut up, bitch. You enticed me to this car, and you want to fuck me. Your husband thinks he's something special. He's not. You're not. I'll show you what a real man can do." Komal ripped through her panties and lifted her leg. He grabbed her hair with the other, and she pushed at him ineffectively. “No, stop! I don’t want this!”

He crushed her mouth with his. She could feel the bile in her stomach rise, but that was where she needed him. He turned and slid his hips down, then bit her shoulder.

She grabbed the heel of her shoe as he centered over her. Val twisted violently. “Bitch, hold still.” Komal lifted to one arm, trying to grab her hip. She slid the needle out of her shoe. Komal caught her arm and slammed it back to the floor. “What is this?” He glared at the needle.

Val slammed her forehead into his nose and lifted her legs, wrapping them around his neck. She flipped him to his back and hammered his cock and balls with a fist. He screamed in rage yet couldn’t prevent the convulsive, protective curl his body demanded. Val disengaged, rolling to the right. She regained her balance and slammed back on top of the fucker. She didn’t have the time or energy for finesse. She shoved the needle through the bottom of his chin and upward. He thrashed, grasping at his face. Val slid the other needle out from her heel and grabbed the fuckers face.

“This is for every child you hurt, you son of a bitch.” She rammed the needle through the bastard's eye and stirred the razor-sharp shard scrambling the fucker's brain like eggs. Then she released the acid held in the tube.

Val panted and pushed herself up, straddling Komal as his body went through the process of dying now that his brain wasn't sending impulses for it to continue. She put her hand to her ear. She heard Smith grunt and release a hiss of expelled air. She stood up and moved away from Komal. Kicking off her shoes, she bolted to the door. She had to help Smith.

~

SMITHSON STOOD AFTER THE HAND. "If you'll excuse me."

"Where are you going?" Blanton asked as all three men looked up at him.

"I'll be back." He moved before another word could be said. He heard Val give him the location. They were in the luggage car, and he was heading that way. He made it to the second sleeper car before he saw Komal's men hustling through the first. Smith casually walked through the kitchen car listening as Val pleaded with that bastard to stop. He bolted into the supply car and reached the end when Blanton called after him.

He turned in time to see the knife launch out of No Name's hand. Smith dropped into a crouch, and the knife flew past him, embedding itself in the insulated wall of the supply car. He stood and grabbed the knife out from the wall. He had a gun, and he'd use it if necessary, but they needed time, and a gunshot would draw unneeded attention.

Smith lifted his free hand and beckoned them forward. "Let's go." He dropped into a fighting position. Blanton drew a knife, as did Sam, but Smith could tell it would be Mr. No Name who would move on him first. Blanton tossed his knife to the bastard, and the other two stepped back. Smith watched and waited. *Left foot first. Left-handed hold on the knife*. Smith had been in more than his share of knife fights in back alleys. He waited for the bastard to make his move. The ass was too impatient. He'd lunge first. As expected, the man advanced and slashed in a wide arc. Nobody who wanted to live on the streets fought that way. Smith didn't feign or move. He blocked the wide swing with his arm and stabbed hard and fast. One, two, three, four times. He backed away, and No Name dropped to his knees. The look of complete surprise on his opponent's face vanished as he flopped to the floor.

Smith stood and walked forward. Sam looked nervously at Blanton, who lifted his chin and ordered Sam into action. Smith didn't stop walking. Sam sidestepped and sprung at him, but Smith twisted, smacked Sam's attempted stab away, and rammed the knife into Sam's throat. The action barely paused his progress to Blanton.

Blanton lifted his hands into fists and started moving his feet like a boxer. Smith pushed forward, and Blanton slammed a punch into his gut while swinging an uppercut to his head. The gut punch pushed a hiss of air out of him. Smith blocked the uppercut and grabbed Blanton's shirt pulling him forward and off his balance. Then Smith lifted the bastard above his head and threw him against a wooden vegetable bin. Blanton screamed in pain, his hands contorted into misshaped claws as his body spasmed. Smith smiled. He'd broken the fucker's back. He grabbed Blanton by the shirt collar and headed to the door leading to the luggage car. The door flew open, and he crouched, reaching for his weapon, still holding Blanton by the shirt collar.

Val stood in the doorway. White hair flying in

the wind, crouched and ready for a fight. The woman was naked as the day was long and smeared in blood. She saw him and turned to take in the scene around her before slowly lifting upright. “What are you going to do with him?”

“Send a signal,” Smith said. “Are you hurt? Did he ...”

Val lifted her chin. “No. The bastard’s dead. It wasn’t pretty, and there’s a mess to clean up.”

Smith dragged Blanton to her and dropped him before he took off his jacket and handed it to her. “Go back to the room. I’ll take care of the cleanup.”

“No. The job isn’t done.” She put the jacket on and buttoned it up before putting her hands on her hips. “We’re a team.”

Smith knew they had a finite amount of time before someone would retire to the staff’s quarters and find them. “Meat hooks.” He nodded to the refrigerated vault. Val was on it as he dragged the whimpering Blanton to the transition area between railroad cars. Val skittered to a stop at the door and handed him an iron hook. “What are you going to do?”

“Get rid of evidence and send a signal.”

He dropped Blanton to the floor. Grabbing the

hook in his hand, he lifted it above his head and rammed it into Blanton's abdomen, shoving the hook through the man's rib cage. "Ew. Warn a woman, will you," Val said from behind him. She flicked off some fresh blood from her face.

Smith couldn't help the chuff of laughter. He grabbed ahold of the ladder and dragged Blanton up after him, then slid the now dead man to the side of the car and wedged the handle of the meat hook into a metal pole anchored lengthways into the top of the car. He kicked Blanton's body over the side. In the dark, no one would see the body. No one except Harbinger when he was looking for a sign in the early morning light.

Val was at the top of the ladder, watching him. "I'll get three more meat hooks." As she disappeared from the ladder, he stood up, panting from the effort it took to haul Blanton's dead weight up the ladder. The moon and stars shone with the brilliance of a million points of light. The cool air rushed across his hot skin, and he rolled his shoulders. He was no longer a hired killer, a murderer, and a criminal. He had a higher purpose. He would spend his life defending those who had no protector, hunting down and killing the monsters of the world. This time he'd killed for the right reason, and the difference was legion. The weight of his past life lifted like dust and floated away on the breeze caused by the slow-moving train. For the first time in his life, he belonged, mattered to someone, and had a purpose. Smith moved to the ladder. There was still work to do.

18

Val walked in front of Smith as they slowly made their way over the roof of the kitchen car. They'd moved the bodies and hastily cleaned the blood from the floors using the materials found in the supply car. All evidence, including her shredded dress and shoes, was pitched off the train.

The kitchen staff below them laughed and drank as they cleaned for the night, or perhaps they were prepping for the morning meal. The skylights in the kitchen car gave both her and Smith the intel they needed. The staff was relaxed, so the parade of people through the kitchen was nothing new. Interesting, but Val didn't have the energy to wonder why. She'd accept the gift. They made their way from car to car. She chuckled as she thought of the movies where the heroes and bad guys jumped from car to car as the train moved. Ridiculous and risky. They used the ladder to go down, crossed the transition, and climbed up the next car. At their sleeping car, Smith entered the hall first and made his way to their quarters. He blocked the hallway with his frame, and she sprinted down the hall and into the small compartment. It would be tough to explain her wearing only his coat and splattered in smeared blood.

She waited for him to shut the door and dropped into his big body, completely exhausted. His arms came around her, and they stood like that, rocking gently with the train for several minutes. "I've never had this. Someone to ... decompress with." She sighed and arched her back, staring up at him. "You have impressive skills."

Smith didn't say anything for a moment. "Did he hurt you? You know what I mean." He moved the lapel of his jacket and traced the bruise forming around the bite mark on her chest.

Val shook her head. "I played the victim until I could get to my weapons, then it was game over."

"I saw the evidence of the end game when I drove a meat hook through his chest." His lip twitched upward. "I hated hearing what was happening."

She wrapped her arms around his neck. "Is it wrong that I like you hating it?"

"No." He bent down and kissed her, almost reverently. "Go, shower. I want him off you."

Val nodded. So did she. She showered quickly but scrubbed where Komal's hands had touched her with extra effort. They switched places, and Smith showered while she dressed in blue jeans, a navy sweater, and running shoes. She pulled her hair up into a high ponytail and spun it into a bun, pinning it into place. On their run from the train, she'd cover her hair with a cap. Val laid out his clothes for him and watched as he dressed. His body was magnificent, and she'd never tire of looking at him. Or being with him, for that matter. He was a rock of stability, kindness, and support. She'd hold on to him with every iota of strength she possessed because she'd been floating without solid ground under her feet for far too long.

As Smith tied his shoes, he asked, "How much time do we have?"

"Not long now. We should rest while we can."

"Good plan." He sat down and held out his hand. She moved from where she was onto the bed with him and leaned her head on his shoulder. He lifted his feet, stretching his long legs across the aisle. Val threaded her fingers through his. "You're an amazing man."

He sighed and squeezed her hand gently. "I could be."

She smiled in the dimly lit interior of the sleeping quarters. "You are. To me, you are. I don't want to lose this." She let that vulnerability slip out. It was a calculated risk, but she prayed he felt the same way.

"Then we won't." His words were a statement of fact. So like Smith. Black and white, no gray, no blurring of the lines he'd defined in his brilliant mind.

She popped her head up and looked at him. "How did you think of the signal?"

He glanced down at her. "A movie I once watched. I think it was a spy movie."

She smiled and laughed. Smith's low rumble of laughter filled the cabin, too. He patted her arm. "Are you ready?"

She nodded and stood up. At least that time, when they walked on the roofs of the railway cars, she'd have tennis shoes on. She extended her hand to him. "Let's finish this."

~

"What signal are we looking for?" Hoss asked as they watched the speck of a train. Harbinger shrugged, not taking his eyes off the horizon. "Knowing those two, it could be anything." The Oscar Team leader grunted and shifted in his lean against the porch.

"Think there's food on that train?" Squirrel, the smallest man on the team, asked from where he was sitting cross-legged on top of a junction box, looking through binoculars.

"Damn it, Squirrel. You just ate." Ramp tossed a stick at his teammate. There was no need to be quiet. There was absolutely nothing and nobody near them. The one man who lived in the shack they were outside of, obviously the employee who pulled the switch for the train, was sleeping thanks to a syringe full of knock-out juice that Hoot, the team's medic, administered.

Harbinger liked the guys. Ramp reached out and tapped Halo on the shoulder. They both studied the train through sniper scopes. "You seeing what I'm seeing?"

Halo lifted his head and then dropped to the scope again. He spoke while looking through the scope, "Yo, Harbinger. Could four dead men hanging off one of the railroad cars be your signal?"

Well, shit, that was not Val's style. His opinion of Smithson leveled up about twenty notches. That was a hell of a statement. Hell of a signal, too. "No doubt about it. Throw the switch."

Ramp, Halo, and Hoot jogged across the tracks and threw the switch, moving one set of tracks into the other. "They'll have to slow down, but we'll still have to hustle." Hoss looked at him. "Recovered enough from that horse ride to run?"

Harbinger flipped off Oscar Team's leader, and Squirrel cackled from where he sat. "I ain't never seen anyone ride that poorly. I felt sorry for that horse." Hoss chuckled.

"I hate horses," Harbinger grumbled.

"Dude, they hate you, too." Hoss laughed. "If you ever want to learn how to ride, my old man has a horse ranch in Kentucky. He raises thoroughbreds. He's my fucking hero. Built the ranch from the ground up. He'll teach you how to ride or get one of his people to do it."

Squirrel pointed to the train. "Ah, damn. Now I see them. Dude, they look like they've been put on hooks. They're flopping like dead fish on a stringer." He handed Harbinger the binoculars. He found the car and the bodies and focused the binoculars as the train approached and slowed. "That's Komal." He scanned the rest of the bodies. *Don't recognize that one, or... Nope, no idea who that was ...* "That's Blanton. Mission complete. Now we get our people the hell out of Dodge. Or Russia."

"We're in Mongolia," Hoss reminded him.

He slapped the binoculars into Hoss' chest. "Whatever."

"Wherever, actually," Squirrel corrected him as he jumped down from the junction box.

"Screw all of you. Ready to run?" Harbinger laughed and slipped on his backpack as the rest of the team did the same.

"Front of the train." Halo pointed. "Someone is hanging off that car. This one is big, and he's definitely alive," he amended.

Harbinger glanced up. "He's ours. That's our up point, gents." They all trotted toward the rail. "Let's go." Harbinger turned and sprinted as the locomotive hummed past. He reached out, and Smithson literally pulled him up to the step. He hustled up and watched the giant man swing each team member up. Squirrel, the second to last up, damn near flew over Smithson's shoulder. Hoss clasped hands with Smithson, and the team was on board. Harbinger looked around. "Where's Val?"

~

SMITH POINTED UP THE LADDER. "She's in the locomotive, ensuring the engineer doesn't change his mind and hit the brakes." He glanced at the team. "Someone needs to relieve her."

Hoss turned to Halo. "Make it happen. No stopping. Period."

"On it." The man climbed the ladder and was gone seconds later.

"Status?" Harbinger asked him.

Smith started up the ladder. "Blanton and Komal are dead."

"Yeah, we saw. Hell of a signal, by the way. Who were the other two?" Harbinger asked as he followed him. Smith looked back when he stood on top of the slow-moving train. Hoss and the rest of his team followed them up the ladder.

"They worked for Komal." Smithson shrugged. "If we get the staff out of this car, we can uncouple it and let the rest of the train stop."

"What about cell phones?" Hoss asked. "They could call ahead."

"No service," Smith said as they stood on top of the train.

"That doesn't mean they don't have access to a Satellite phone or Ham radio. There has to be some way for emergency communication even out here. The people in this country aren't in the stone age, and more and more of these villages are getting internet." Hoss put his hands on his hips. "We need to ensure there's no way for them to communicate."

Harbinger turned to him. "How many people are on the train?"

"Twenty-three passengers, half that in staff. They aren't at full occupancy." Smith rattled off the information.

"We push the staff back, pull the passengers out of their room, and take them to the back, to a single car. Hoss, you, and your team search the cars after we clear them. We'll hold them in the back until you're done." Harbinger turned to him. "Are you carrying?"

Smith lifted his sweater, exposing his weapon. He waited while Hoss and his team decided who would do what. When they were ready, he led the way.

He opened the door to the crew's sleeping quarters, and as quietly as possible, he and Harbinger opened doors and rousted people. Several of the rooms were vacant but obviously lived in. “Cooks,” he muttered to Harbinger. The man nodded as they shoved the terrified crew into motion. Daria looked at him like he’d killed her puppy. He pushed her toward the rest of the crew. Harbinger led while he motivated from the rear, holding a weapon on the crew as they advanced through the luggage to the supply car. “Kitchen car. Get the staff. I’ll give you one minute.” Smith motioned to Harbinger.

Harbinger jogged toward the car, and Smith did a slow count to sixty before he ordered the staff forward. Harbinger was at the door and had the kitchen staff on their knees, shaking and terrified. “Get up!” Harbinger hissed in Russian, and they pushed the staff onward. They used the same process in the passenger cars.

Smith gathered people, shoving them out into the hall. A gun in the face silenced them all too quickly. He opened a door and found his parents. "Get up and get out." He spoke in Russian, the barrel of his weapon pushed against his father's temple.

His father hissed, "Komal will kill you for this."

"He'll have to find his way out of hell first," Smith hissed and grabbed his mother, shaking her awake. He pulled her from the bed and shoved her to his father. "Move."

They passed through the game car, into the dining room, and then to the bar car. Harbinger yelled at everyone to go to their knees.

"Why are you doing this? Are you robbing us?" One of the women sobbed, and her husband hushed her.

Harbinger laughed. "No. You just picked the wrong train, lady."

Smith's mom snorted. "No, you did. This train is carrying Bratva. My family will find you and kill you for this."

It was Smith's turn to laugh. "Family means that much to you?"

"Family is everything. I am Nadia Solntesevskaya. You're as good as dead."

"You're an outcast. You've only started to repair your reputation with the family, which is probably why you were tasked with escorting Komal to Beijing. A menial job that the lowest foot soldier could perform. No wonder you hated him," Smith growled the words.

Both of his parents paled. Smith pulled the hammer back on his weapon. The metallic click was deafening in the quiet of the railcar. Harbinger cleared his throat, "Dude, they aren't sanctioned."

"I'm not going to kill them." Smith smiled. "But I will find out why they were traveling with Komal. Why is the Bratva interested in a man who uses children to wage war? Or is it the sex trade that the Bratva is interested in?"

His mother's eyes closed, and she turned her head at that comment. His father looked down. So, it was the sex trade they were involved with. "Komal is dead. He died under your escort. No one will be pleased, not the Bratva and not the people he was meeting in Beijing."

Hoss opened the door. "Smith, H, we're done. Two sat phones and a radio. All are destroyed."

"Smith! I knew you'd turn out this way," his mother hissed. "You're just like your father."

His father's head jerked, and he hissed, "He isn't mine. He's just like that bastard you slept with.

He's bloodthirsty, just like him. I told you he would be."

His mother threw back her head and laughed almost manically, and Smith put a bullet through the roof, silencing everything. "We have a sharp-shooter watching this train. If anyone leaves this car, you're dead." He backed out after Harbinger and closed the door.

They sprinted to the front of the train, where Hoss' team was ready to decouple the cars from the front of the train. Smith walked across the transition and stood beside Val. They watched as the team uncoupled the car, and the rest of the train slowed. Harbinger clapped a hand on his arm. "If those were your parents, you're better off without them."

He didn't say a word. No wonder his father had turned him out. Events from his life started falling into place. The reason he didn't look like his father or his sisters and only minimally like his mother had been explained. When the others left, he moved behind Val and circled her waist with his arms. She leaned back into him. His eyes held the horizon until the disconnected cars were nothing but a memory.

Val turned in his arms and looked up at him. "Are you ready to start the rest of your life?"

Smith stared down at her. *Was he? God, yes.* He glanced back at the horizon and spoke the truth, "I've waited a lifetime for this moment."

19

Smith stared out the window of the luxury apartment he now occupied with Val. He was still amazed at how his life had changed in the last few months. He watched the flashing lights from the Christmas tree twinkling in the corner of the large living room and allowed a smile to form. Val was a force of nature. She'd seen something in him that no one else, including himself, had seen. She said he was her rock, her steadying force, but in reality, the woman was his salvation.

"What are you doing up so early?" Val padded across the floor and almost fell into him. He wrapped her up in his arms.

"It's Christmas." He couldn't recall when he'd

been that happy or content. He was excited about the holiday for the first time in his life.

Val leaned back and narrowed her eyes at him. "Barely?"

He smiled and dropped a kiss on her lips. She smiled up at him. "Come to bed, and I'll give you your first Christmas present."

He dropped a kiss on her lips. "Go ahead. I'll be there in a minute."

She narrowed her eyes. "Are you sure?"

"I am." He kissed her again, extending the contact, letting his tongue dance with hers.

When the kiss ended, she purred and ran her hand over his stiff cock. "Don't be long." She slid out of his arms, and he watched as she ghosted out of the room, her pale cream silk nightgown floating around her. He didn't deserve her and could never be worthy of the woman who'd literally given him his life back. He walked to the tree and bent down, moving packages until he found the one he wanted. Smithson slipped it into the pocket of his silk pajama bottoms and made his way into the bedroom.

Val had shed her nightgown. He walked to the side of the bed, carefully dropped his pajama bottoms, so the box in the pocket wouldn't make a sound, and kneed onto the bed. He lay between her legs and dropped down to kiss the woman he loved.

He trailed kisses down her neck to her breast and paid attention to the hard tip of her nipple. Val urged him lower, but he had other ideas. He started again at her mouth and then down the other side of her neck. She arched under him, silently pleading for more.

Smith granted her wish and kissed lower, moving slowly as his tongue painted a trail to her sex. Val's hands tangled in his hair and her hips lifted against his mouth as he lowered. God, the sounds the woman made boiled his blood. Her soft moans, panted pleas, and quiet gasps were the delicious bits he devoured, but they only left him starving for more. These moments were when Val was completely his. When the jobs, the world, and the life they led wasn't begging for attention. There they were completely vulnerable, something neither of them usually allowed themselves to be. He kissed each thigh and lifted to his knees, pulling her down the bed toward him. Her hair spread like a halo above her. "You are beautiful." He couldn't resist dropping down and kissing her.

Val caressed his cheek and stared up at him. "I

love you."

It wasn't the first time she'd said the words, but like the first time, his breath caught, and he internalized the intensity and the meaning. He dropped and kissed her again and then whispered, "I love you more."

He entered her, repeating the words in his mind, or perhaps he said them out loud. It didn't matter. Val was his life, his love, and his salvation. His hips found the fast and deep rhythm that she loved. Her body slowly tightened as he drove them both to their release. They fell over the edge almost simultaneously. He caught himself on his elbows and dropped his head to the pillow beside hers.

Val's fingers trailed over his skin, sending shivers of sensation through his limbs. "Merry Christmas." She kissed his shoulder.

He dropped to his side, and she cuddled into him. "Merry Christmas. That was a wonderful present."

She laughed. "That wasn't the present." She rolled and moved over to her side table. "This is the present."

She handed him a small box. It looked suspiciously like the box he had for her. He reached down to retrieve his and sat up facing her. She looked at the box in her hand and then the one in his. "Did we have the same idea?" She laughed and turned, moving to sit in his lap. "Let's open them at the same time?"

"Deal."

Val counted down. "Three, two, one."

They opened the packages at the same time. He opened the lid of his, and she opened hers. "Oh, God." She put her hand over her mouth. "Really?"

He smiled and turned his box to her. "Really?"

Val laughed. "Someone should probably pop the question."

Smith dropped his chin onto her shoulder. "Will you marry me?"

Val took the pale blue diamond solitaire out of the black box and handed it to him, holding her left hand up. He slid the ring onto her finger.

She picked up the silver and diamond band she'd bought him and slipped it on his finger. "I will marry you, Smith. I most definitely will marry you." She hugged him, and he flopped back onto the mattress. All those years of suffering were over. His Norse warrior angel and savior, his Valkyrie, had chosen him.

EPILOGUE

Flack grabbed his gun from the nightstand and quietly moved to the door. No one should be at his place, especially that early. He checked the drive and frowned in confusion. Dropping the weapon to his side, he pulled back the curtain to make sure it was who he thought it was.

He opened the door. "Smoke? What the fuck, dude?"

"Can I come in?" Smoke looked too damn serious, and that sent shockwaves through his system. He opened the door and beckoned his mentor inside.

"What's wrong? What happened?"

"I got a call from social services. It's Brooke."

Flack jolted. His niece? "What?"

"Seems your sister Trisha's in-laws have been neglecting her. Social Services were called and given an anonymous tip. They investigated and took Brooke away from them. She's in the hospital. Malnutrition and other things."

Flack dropped into the chair. "What other things?"

"Diaper rash that has festered and gotten infected. RSV, which they said is being treated."

"What the fuck is RSV?"

"A coughing-lung thing that young kids get."

"Son of a bitch. They said they wanted her. You heard them. You were there."

"Yeah. This ain't on you, bud. Anyway, social services said she'll be okay, but they won't return her to them, but they do want to place her with family. That's you."

"With me?" Flack sprung up, his gun still in his hand as he spun. The sleek glass, concrete, and metal home was a multi-level work of modern art. Sharp edges were accentuated with stark white decor punctuated with bold pops of color. "Look at this place. It is more of a museum than a house. This isn't a place for a baby. I'm gone for months on end. I … I'm an assassin, for fuck's sake. Who in their right mind would leave a little girl with me?" He stopped and stared at Smoke. Cold, stark fear ran through him. "I don't know anything about raising a baby."

"Most people don't." Smoke handed him a slip of paper. "Here's the number for the social worker. Brooke is at the pediatric unit at Methodist. Before you tell them you can't take care of her, see your niece and ensure she's okay. They have programs for this type of situation. Foster homes and such. Your sister would have wanted you to ensure her baby was okay."

Flack nodded and took the paper. Smoke walked to the door and turned around. "Merry Christmas, Flack. Go see your niece."

Flack listened to Smoke's vehicle start and leave. Still, he stood in the middle of his living room and stared at the series of digits on the paper. The only living connection to anyone he had on this planet was in the hospital. Because the people he'd left her with neglected her.

Dear God, what was he going to do?

IF YOU'D LIKE to read Flack's Story, click here!

ALSO BY KRIS MICHAELS

Kings of the Guardian Series

Jacob: Kings of the Guardian Book 1

Joseph: Kings of the Guardian Book 2

Adam: Kings of the Guardian Book 3

Jason: Kings of the Guardian Book 4

Jared: Kings of the Guardian Book 5

Jasmine: Kings of the Guardian Book 6

Chief: The Kings of Guardian Book 7

Jewell: Kings of the Guardian Book 8

Jade: Kings of the Guardian Book 9

Justin: Kings of the Guardian Book 10

Christmas with the Kings

Drake: Kings of the Guardian Book 11

Dixon: Kings of the Guardian Book 12

Passages: The Kings of Guardian Book 13

Promises: The Kings of Guardian Book 14

The Siege: Book One, The Kings of Guardian Book 15

The Siege: Book Two, The Kings of Guardian Book 16

A Backwater Blessing: A Kings of Guardian Crossover Novella

Montana Guardian: A Kings of Guardian Novella

Guardian Defenders Series

Gabriel

Maliki

John

Jeremiah

Frank

Guardian Security Shadow World

Anubis (Guardian Shadow World Book 1)

Asp (Guardian Shadow World Book 2)

Lycos (Guardian Shadow World Book 3)

Thanatos (Guardian Shadow World Book 4)

Tempest (Guardian Shadow World Book 5)

Smoke (Guardian Shadow World Book 6)

Reaper (Guardian Shadow World Book 7)

Phoenix (Guardian Shadow World Book 8)

Valkyrie (Guardian Shadow World Book 9)

Flack (Guardian Shadow World Book 10)

Hollister (A Guardian Crossover Series)

Andrew (Hollister-Book 1)

Zeke (Hollister-Book 2)

Hope City

Hope City - Brock

HOPE CITY - Brody- Book 3

Hope City - Ryker - Book 5

Hope City - Killian - Book 8

Hope City - Blayze - Book 10

The Long Road Home

Season One:

My Heart's Home

Season Two:

Searching for Home (A Hollister-Guardian Crossover Novel)

STAND ALONE NOVELS

SEAL Forever - Silver SEALs

A Heart's Desire - Stand Alone

Hot SEAL, Single Malt (SEALs in Paradise)

Hot SEAL, Savannah Nights (SEALs in Paradise)

Hot SEAL, Silent Knight (SEALs in Paradise)

ABOUT THE AUTHOR

Wall Street Journal and USA Today Bestselling Author, Kris Michaels is the alter ego of a happily married wife and mother. She writes romance, usually with characters from military and law enforcement backgrounds.

Made in the USA
Coppell, TX
16 November 2022

86499935R00173